The Vampire's Visit

David A. Poulsen

KEY PORTER BOOKS

Library and Archives Canada Cataloguing in Publication

Poulsen, David A., 1946–
The Vampire's Visit / David A. Poulsen.

(Salt & Pepper chronicles)
ISBN 1-55263-721-2

1. Vampires—Juvenile fiction. I. Title. II. Series.

PS8581.O848V3 2006 JC813'.54 C2005-906556-7

The publisher gratefully acknowledges the support of the Canada Council for the Arts and the Ontario Arts Council for its publishing program. We acknowledge the support of the Government of Ontario through the Ontario Media Development Corporation's Ontario Book Initiative.

We acknowledge the financial support of the Government of Canada through the Book Publishing Industry Development Program (BPIDP) for our publishing activities.

An earlier version of this book was published by Roussan Publishers Inc. in 1996.

Key Porter Books Limited
Six Adelaide Street East, Tenth Floor
Toronto, Ontario
Canada M5C 1H6

www.keyporter.com

Text design and formatting: Ingrid Paulson/Martin Gould

Printed and bound in Canada

06 07 08 09 10 5 4 3 2 1

To the Yu family

Much of this was written at a table
near the back of their restaurant—
the Four Winds Café—in Longview, Alberta.
Thanks for the coffee and the encouragement.

Bound for Jolly Olde England

It started with garlic.

Garlands of garlic, like holly at Christmas time. Except it wasn't Christmas. And it wasn't holly. It was garlic. And it was hanging over the windows and doors of Mr. Peter Cubbington-Smith's house. Which except for the garlic was a beautiful home on the edge of London. That's London, England.

Well, actually, I guess it started before the garlic. The whole thing *really* began when Pepper McKenzie's parents decided to spend the summer in England. Then, because I'm Pepper's best friend, they invited me to go along. That was the good part.

Let me tell you about Pepper McKenzie. Pepper's real name is Patti, but the only person who calls her that is her mom. When Pepper was little, her dad called her

Peppermint Patti after a character in the *Peanuts* cartoon (dads are weird). Eventually the Peppermint Patti thing got shortened to Peppermint and finally Pepper. I think if I was Pepper the nickname would drive me nuts, but she doesn't seem to mind.

Pepper has red hair, beautiful skin, an awesome smile and green eyes that light up at the mere thought of anything that could be called an adventure. That's the part I can't totally figure out. I like adventures in movies or books, but not so much in real life. Yet I'm best friends with an excitement freak. Looking back on things, that's probably why we got involved in the mystery in the first place. It was certainly not something I ever thought would happen to me.

Anyway, Pepper and I have known each other since we were six years old. That's when her family moved to Riverbend. We met at a community picnic not long after the McKenzies arrived and we've been best buds ever since. Even though Pepper lives in town and I live in the country and she loves excitement and I love peace and quiet, we get along really well. Most of the time.

So, as I was saying, our parents had agreed that the two of us would be going to England. Cool. At that point, however, temporary insanity apparently took hold of everyone (except me), and my dweeb brother, Hal, the ten-year-old version of the Creature from the Black Lagoon, got invited to go along too. The adults—Pepper's parents and mine—felt it would be bad for Hal's self-esteem if his sister, meaning me, got to go to England for the summer and he didn't. *That* was definitely the bad part.

By the way, my name is Christine Louise Bellamy, although most of the time I'm called Salt. That's what you get for hanging around with someone called Pepper, I guess. Salt and Pepper. Cute, isn't it?

To be honest, my life is pretty good. I'm twelve years old. I'm well fed, I live in an okay house in an okay town and I just passed seventh grade. I'd like to be prettier, a lot prettier, but my mom says to be patient, that I will be. She keeps telling me that. I've decided to give her the benefit of the doubt. Of course, that doesn't stop me from checking the mirror five or six times a day to see if her prediction is coming true. So far, I'd say it isn't. What I see every time I look in that mirror is straight brown hair, a face that makes my cheeks kind of stand out and a mouth that makes me look mad even when I'm not.

Speaking of parents, I guess I should tell you about mine. They're . . . well . . . parents. I mean, what can you say about people whose idea of a good time is to have this party once a year where everybody dresses in red clothes, wears lots of red makeup, and drinks tomato juice drinks and eats tomato-type food. Then they sit around watching this ancient movie, *Attack of the Killer Tomatoes*, laughing like it's the funniest thing they've ever seen.

My parents have had about four of those parties now, which is pretty strange, too. I mean, wouldn't one tomato party be enough? But, basically, except for a few bizarre things like that, my parents are all right.

Then, of course, there's my sister, Janet. Ever since she started high school, she doesn't actually talk to anyone else in the family, except to whine or complain. Most of the time the whining and complaining is about me, which is why I was really glad my parents didn't decide to send Janet to England too. They probably figured her self-esteem was okay.

Which brings me back to Hal. You'll notice a certain similarity between my little brother's name and that place where the devil lives. This is not mere coincidence. Hal is short and his face is round and pink. It's the kind of face that adults think is cute. People who know better—like me—realize it is just totally annoying.

So there I was, about to spend two whole months in the land of Charles Dickens, Oasis, Shakespeare, Sherlock Holmes, Coldplay and royalty. With Hal. I guess you could say I had mixed emotions about the trip.

You're Kidding, Right?

One thing I should explain right off is that I don't believe in vampires. Or at least I didn't. Actually, I didn't know very much about them, which is why one of the first things I did when I arrived at Mr. Peter Cubbington-Smith's was to ask him right out, "Why do you have all this garlic everywhere?" He even had some hanging around his neck.

I'd read somewhere that certain people think garlic will keep you from getting a cold, but this man had enough garlic around the place to keep all of London free from germs.

The place, by the way, was something else. It was huge, a country manor with acres of perfectly trimmed lawns and hedges, and thoroughbred horses grazing peacefully in a green pasture not far from the house. There was a tree-lined lane that ran from the front door to the main road, which was about a five-minute bike ride away. Let me tell you, that's a lot of trees.

The house itself wasn't really a house. It was more like a castle. Without the moat. And the moat was about the only thing the place was missing. It had turrets and parapets and nooks and crannies and vines on most of the walls. There must have been about a hundred walls. And doors and windows everywhere. As soon as I saw the place, I figured there were too many doors for all of them to actually *go* someplace. Some were probably there just for show. As if that wasn't weird enough on its own, there was that thing with the garlic. Every one of the windows and doors had giant garlands of garlic hanging over them. Well, almost every one. I'll get to that later.

To be honest, I kind of figured that Mr. Peter Cubbington-Smith was strange. Which was maybe a little unfair, but you can see how somebody might think that. Mr. Cubbington-Smith had been a colonel in the English army. He told us that while we were driving into London from Gatwick Airport in a car about half a block long. I got the impression that Mr. Cubbington-Smith was pretty well off. It turns out he and Pepper's father went to school together at the University of Edinburgh. I didn't know Mr. McKenzie had ever been to Scotland, but then I guess there's a lot of stuff we don't know about our parents and our friends' parents.

Anyway, I was enjoying the ride. It was the first time I'd ever ridden in a car driven by a chauffeur. I'm pretty sure it was Pepper's first time, too, but she was acting like it was the sort of thing that happened every day. Pepper is like that sometimes.

Whenever we passed somebody on the street she'd do this thing with her hand like she was backhanding flies in slow motion.

"What's that?" I asked after she'd done it about twenty times.

"What's what?"

"That thing you're doing with your hand."

"It's my queen wave. I'm feeling quite royal today."

I looked at her. "You might be feeling royal, but you look stupid."

She didn't bother to answer me. She just kept on backhanding flies. But that was better than what my brother was up to. Hal had whined until they let him sit up front with the chauffeur. Which was weird already because the driver sits on the right in English cars and the cars travel on the left side of the road. Anyway, there was Hal, sitting where the driver normally goes in North American cars. He had his window rolled down and he was yelling to people, "Howdy! I'm from Canada! My name's Mario Lemieux!"

Every once in a while, for variety I guess, he'd introduce himself as Jarome Iginla. I felt sorry for the people who were walking along minding their own business only to find themselves face to face with a fake hockey star and Queen Flyswatter the First.

I couldn't stand watching them for one more minute, so I turned my attention to the conversation between Mr. Cubbington-Smith and the McKenzies. It was boring—stories about stuff they'd done years before, the usual adult talk.

That's when I noticed the thing hanging on the string that went around Mr. Cubbington-Smith's neck, which, by the way, was one of the skinniest necks I'd ever seen. At first I thought it must be a strange war medal or something. I waited for a break in the conversation and asked him about it.

"This?" he said, fingering the thing. "It's a clove of garlic."

He didn't say any more, so I figured it must be normal behaviour for English people to wear garlic instead of jewellery. The more I thought about that, the weirder it seemed, so during the next lull in the conversation... "Why are you wearing garlic?" I tried to make my voice sound casual, like I was asking him about the weather. I didn't want him to think I was rude.

"Vampires," he said, like he was telling me it might rain tomorrow.

"Oh," I said.

Pepper stopped waving. "Vampires!" she screeched. Obviously she wasn't worried about being rude.

"Oh yes," Mr. Cubbington-Smith nodded. "They're quite bad right now."

"Oh, I get it," I laughed. "You're talking about mosquitoes, right? Those little bloodsuckers?" I figured it must be some quaint British tradition to refer to mosquitoes as vampires.

"No," Mr. Cubbington-Smith shook his head. "I'm talking about vampires, the *big* bloodsuckers."

There was silence in the car after that. Except for Hal, of course, who hadn't heard our conversation because he and the chauffeur were separated from us by a glass partition. But somehow, we could still hear him.

"Howdy! I'm from Canada!" he yelled to a lady who looked like she might be a nanny. She was pushing a baby carriage. "My name's Sidney Crosbie."

The Vampires of London

It wasn't until we were in the house and sitting in a room the size of our school gym that Pepper got all curious about the vampires. "You don't really believe in them, do you—vampires, I mean?" she asked Mr. Cubbington-Smith.

Actually you could have played Frisbee in there, the room was so large. The furniture was old-fashioned but very expensive looking, and the carpet on the floor was the size of our front lawn back home in Riverbend. There were paintings of people in costumes on the walls. All of them had skinny necks, too, so I figured maybe they were Cubbington-Smith ancestors. Even though you knew that a lot of money had been spent on decorating, it wasn't stuffy like a lot of expensive places. In fact, with the fire blazing away in a huge stone fireplace in one corner of the room, it was actually kind of cozy.

Mr. Cubbington-Smith lifted his eyebrows and stared down his long, pointed nose at Pepper. "Dear girl, if one says one believes or doesn't believe in something, there is an indication that the thing one believes or doesn't believe in is in doubt. In this case, there is no doubt. There are vampires. I have seen them and I have seen the results of their work. And, I take the necessary precautions."

"But vampires don't live here in London, do they?" asked Mr. McKenzie. He was leaning forward and he looked sort of amused. I don't think he could believe that his old friend was serious. "I thought vampires only inhabited places with foreign-sounding names—like Transylvania."

"Ah, the moving pictures," Mr. Cubbington-Smith smiled. "Mustn't be fooled by that, old man. I have, as I mentioned, seen a number of vampires and only a few have looked like Count Dracula of the movies. Even fewer have fangs—although some do have rather pronounced canine teeth—and none have spoken with that dreadful accent... 'I vant to drink your blodd.'" Mr. Cubbington-Smith smiled.

"But Peter," Mrs. McKenzie frowned, "surely you're joking—a story to amuse the children?"

"No," Mr. Cubbington-Smith shook his head firmly. "It is no joke, I assure you."

"When can we meet one?" You can guess where that question came from.

"I would hope that you will not meet one." Our host looked at my brother, then lowered his voice. "Although it is not impossible. They are very active right now."

"You mean they come around more often at certain times of the year?" I asked. "Like vegetables in season?" I thought I was being pretty cute with that bit.

"I figured they'd be hungry all the time," Pepper added.

"Not so, actually." Mr. Cubbington-Smith leaned back in his huge armchair and reached into his pocket for his pipe. "They are quite inactive for long periods, sometimes several weeks. During those periods they will feed rarely, if at all."

"Sort of like bears hibernating for the winter," Pepper snickered and all of us laughed, or at least smiled. Everybody, that is, except Mr. Cubbington-Smith.

He leaned forward and his eyes got small and angry looking. "I'm afraid I am quite unwilling to view all of this in a humorous way. We are talking about creatures—dead creatures who refuse to stay dead—that go about killing by draining their victims' blood."

"None of us is making fun of what you're telling us, Peter," Mr. McKenzie told his friend. "It's just that we've always thought that the myths about vampires were just that—myths."

Mr. Cubbington-Smith seemed to calm down. He lit his pipe and took a couple of puffs before he spoke. "I quite understand. However, I assure you that they are *not* myths and a failure to take the appropriate precautions is to invite . . . unpleasant consequences."

I was getting a little worried. It was obvious the guy wasn't kidding and he didn't seem to be crazy. But still . . . vampires?

"I . . . uh . . . don't suppose they'll be going into one of those 'inactive' periods any time soon, will they?" I wondered if the others could hear the quiver in my voice. "Like, maybe in the next couple of days?"

"Unfortunately, I think not," our host shook his head. "In fact, I have noticed a recent increase in the frequency of newspaper stories about unsolved murders. For that and other reasons I don't care to discuss, I'm certain that the vampires of London have been keeping quite busy."

The vampires of London. The way Mr. Cubbington-Smith said it made me shudder.

"So we might see one, then." Hal sounded excited about the possibility.

"I wouldn't worry about it if I were you," Pepper told him. "A vampire would have to be pretty desperate to want blood from a total geek."

"Yeah? Well if vampires ate brains, you two would be in no danger at all."

I don't know why my brother included me in his nastiness. I hadn't said or done anything. But, that had never stopped him before.

The way things turned out, I was kind of glad I didn't argue with Hal. He was going to have a couple of bad days. Come to think of it, we all were.

A Weird Manor

The bedroom Pepper and I were sharing was even bigger than the room we'd all been in downstairs. There were three beds, and for a minute I was afraid we might wind up stuck with Hal for a roommate.

But luckily for us he was doing his mature routine and insisted on a room of his own. He ended up two doors down, which was a little strange because there was an empty room between us. We'd noticed it when Mrs. Pudkins, the housekeeper of the manor, was showing us to our rooms after dinner. She acted kind of strange and flustered when we walked past the room separating Hal's room from ours. That's when we asked her about it. First she said it wasn't a bedroom at all, and then she said it was. Finally she looked around and lowered her voice. "We don't use it, haven't for a couple of centuries. It was locked up after . . . well . . . after . . ."

She never did tell us after what. She just made an odd face and scurried past the door.

Pepper and I spent a few minutes getting acquainted with our own room—snooping in the closets and drawers, bouncing on the mattresses and stuff. Finally Pepper stopped and looked at me. "I didn't know England was this weird."

"Me, neither," I told her. "We read all those pamphlets before we came over and not one of them mentioned anything about vampires."

"I know." Pepper sat on one of the beds. "But seriously, maybe this guy is just a nut or something. I mean vampires, locked rooms . . . give me a giant break. Anyway, we're only staying here a week and then we'll be moving on to see how the rest of England lives."

There was a knock at the door—a twerp knock. I'd recognize it anywhere.

"What do you want, Hal?"

"Let me in! Hurry up!" His voice was a sort of excited stage whisper, but with Hal you never know. Ninety percent of the time, he's kidding around, using that sick sense of humour he has.

"Get lost, will ya?" Pepper was beginning to realize what I'd been going through for the past ten years with Hal as a brother.

"C'mon! It's important," he hissed.

I went to the door and let him in. "What do you want, Hal?" I used my "you've got five seconds" voice.

He came into the room, closed the door carefully and looked around for a minute. Then he went and stood by the window. I've seen Hal's goofing around enough times to know when he isn't. He wasn't. He looked scared, or at least nervous.

"Okay, here's the thing," he said. Even when he's scared, my brother likes to be dramatic. "I've just done a little tour of the house. I've been in every room in the place except your parents' room, Mr. Cubbington-Smith's bedroom and the one between us that's locked. There are exactly *two* that don't have garlic over the windows. Mine...," he stepped back with a flourish and pointed, "...and yours."

Sure enough, when Pepper and I looked at the window—we even opened it and stuck our heads out to check—there was no garlic. Things were getting stranger by the minute.

We each sat on one of the beds and looked at the floor, the ceiling, the old furniture in the room, the wallpaper—everything but each other. I guess none of us wanted to admit there could actually be something to this vampire thing.

"Okay, you guys," Pepper finally broke the silence, "if we all agree that this vampire stuff is a load of garbage, then what do we care if there's no garlic on the windows? Unless we're worried about catching a cold or something."

She laughed then, but it wasn't her usual laugh. It was higher and sort of fake, but Hal and I pretended not to notice and joined in.

I guess we were trying to make ourselves feel better. Finally, we agreed that there would be no more talk about vampires.

For the next couple of days we did the rounds of London's tourist stops; you know, the Tower of London, Big Ben, Buckingham Palace, the usual stuff. My favourite part was the Changing of the Guard at the palace. I kept looking around, hoping to see one of the royals, but no luck. Hal loved Madame Tussauds wax museum. He announced halfway through the tour that once he was famous, there'd be a wax version of Hal in there somewhere. I suggested they just pour wax over him and take him now. Pepper wasn't big on all the tourist stuff, but she loved the shopping. She tried to drag us into every clothing store in London. My legs were telling me she almost succeeded. We were having so much fun and we were so busy, we had pretty well put all thoughts of vampires out of our heads.

Until the third night of our stay at the manor, that is. That was the night Simon Chelling stopped by for a visit.

The Visit

It was foggy, one of those London nights like you see in movies. We'd spent the whole day at the Tower of London, which was pretty interesting, especially the Crown Jewels and some of the armour.

Partway through the afternoon, Pepper's parents had a major panic attack because Hal had disappeared. Hal always disappears, so I wasn't particularly worried.

"Shouldn't we look for him?" Mrs. McKenzie sounded upset, which I could understand since the McKenzies were more or less responsible for us while we were in England.

"Nope," Pepper winked at me. "We might find him."

"This isn't funny, Pepper," her dad told her. "Now let's spread out and meet back here in fifteen minutes. I'll stop by Security and let them know he's missing."

"Honestly, I wouldn't worry about it too much, Mr. McKenzie," I tried to reassure him. "He'll pop up somewhere. He's famous for this stuff."

But they insisted and in a few minutes we had spread out and the search was on. I was walking through a room that was full of suits of armour in just about every shape and size. I stopped to look at one outfit that was a little smaller than me. I was trying to figure out if soldiers were really short back then or if the suit was for a medieval midget, when suddenly the arms on the thing came up and grabbed me by the shoulders.

"Infidel!" the armour screamed at me. "You must swear allegiance to the new king or prepare to die!"

I don't know if it was all the stuff about vampires or if I was just nervous being in a strange country—one that is famous for ghosts—but I was one hundred percent sure that some tiny soldier from five hundred years ago was in that armour and that he meant business.

"I... I... uh...," I didn't get past the stammering stage.

"On thy knees, wench, and swear allegiance!" Whoever was in there wasn't to be trifled with, I was sure of that much. I decided it would be best not to irritate the haunted armour any further and sure enough (I hate to admit it now), I got down on one shaky knee. There I was looking up at the freaky metal face; I was all set to cry, I know I was.

"Repeat after me!" the armour ordered.

I nodded meekly.

"Long live King Hal!" the pint-sized knight screeched.

"Long... live...," I started. Then it came to me.

King Hal?

I stood up and stared into the space where the knight's eyes would normally be. Sure enough, there were two brown circles in there, wrinkled up at the corners because the face they were attached to was giggling.

I don't know how he got in there, but Hal was laughing so hard that the armour was making clanking noises. I started yelling at my brother. I was quite loud.

The commotion brought Mr. and Mrs. McKenzie, Pepper, a couple of security guards and several tourists to see what was going on.

The worst part was that, once they all figured out what Hal had done, everybody thought it was hilarious... except the security guards. And even they didn't look nearly as mad as I wanted them to be. I was hoping someone might suggest that Hal should be put into the "bloody tower" for a week or so. A lot of people who spent time there wound up being murdered. Actually, it was pretty awful. There were two princes—Edward and Richard—who were imprisoned in the tower and then killed before Edward could become king. There have been some pretty nasty royals over the centuries.

Pretty soon, there were ten or twelve people standing around listening to Hal's retelling of how he'd tricked me. They were chortling like crazy and behaving like my brother was the best thing Canada had ever sent to England. I walked away wondering if I could get an early flight home.

After the afternoon I'd had, I was hoping for a better evening. Pepper and I were lying on our beds doing a little reading. She was on her stomach, her nose in a Sherlock Holmes story, something about guys with red hair. I was just getting into *Wuthering Heights*. I wasn't sure if I'd made the best choice. It's a love story. I like that, but it's also a little spooky. And I'd had all the scary stuff I needed for one day. Anyway, there I was propped up on two of the thickest, softest pillows I'd ever touched, staring at Chapter Three. Suddenly, it got cold in the room. I looked up to see if Pepper had left the window open.

I knew right away, I'm not sure how. Maybe it was the way he made me feel. It wasn't so much scared as . . . powerless. Shivering cold and miserable—and totally powerless. There was no doubt about it: the creature standing in front of me was a vampire!

He . . . it . . . was standing between Pepper's bed and mine. Mr. Cubbington-Smith was right. He didn't look at all like I thought a vampire would look. Actually, he looked like someone from another time, sort of like the pictures of English gentlemen you see in old novels.

His clothes were old-fashioned but very neat and clean. Still, they looked like most of the dye had been washed out of them. The coat was a faded blue colour and it covered a grey waistcoat. I didn't know the proper names for the clothes he had on, but I found out later. The pantaloons had been green once but were mostly grey now. They disappeared inside tall black boots. The guy had a scarf twisted around his neck but wore no hat. Oh, and there was a cape, a black one, not a bit like a Superman cape.

Maybe it was his skin that gave him away. It was the whitest skin I'd ever seen. He looked like he needed to attend one of my parents' tomato parties. Even his lips had no colour. Only his eyes were different. They were dark, very dark, and always seemed to be looking at you—like those paintings in scary television shows. Even *Scooby-Doo*.

When he spoke, his voice was like his complexion, completely without life or colour. He spoke softly, barely more than a whisper a lot of the time, but it didn't matter. Every time he opened his mouth, it was as if all other sound stopped. You could hear every word.

I was trying to figure out how he just sort of... appeared in the room. I didn't see how he could have got in without either of us noticing. But there he was.

The thing that amazed me was that I wasn't totally terrified. I mean, I was about to get all the blood sucked out of me and I wasn't screaming or crying or anything. I'd read somewhere that vampires often hypnotize their victims so maybe I was a little hypnotized, I don't know. Pepper hadn't freaked either. And Pepper's a freaker, big time.

So, there we were. This guy has suddenly appeared in our room, and both of us are sure he's a vampire and what do we do? We close our books, sit up on our beds and have a chat. Weird, eh?

There are a few other things you should know about this particular vampire. First off, he was very polite.

"How do you do?" he said with a little bow to each of us. "My name is Simon Chelling."

I said, "Good evening," and Pepper said, "Hello, Simon," which is pretty formal for her.

The other interesting thing about our guest was that he was actually quite good looking. In fact, with a little colour, he would have been gorgeous. Oh yeah, and one other point worth mentioning.

Simon Chelling was a teenager—fifteen or sixteen years old at the most.

Good Vampires—Bad Vampires

Pepper and I both put our hands to our necks. I guess we hadn't completely lost sight of who—or what—this stranger was.

The corners of Simon's mouth moved upward ever so slightly as he watched us. Except for one other time it was the closest I ever saw him come to a smile.

"You have, I presume, guessed that I am vampire."

"Yes," I nodded. As our little adventure continued, I noticed that none of the creatures ever used "a" or "the" before the word "vampire" when referring to themselves. I don't know why.

"Uh-huh," Pepper said.

"Then perhaps the first thing I should do is assure you that you are in no danger."

"Oh," we said pretty well together.

"At least, not at the moment."

I figured that meant he wasn't hungry—or is it *thirsty*?—at that exact moment. But later on, when he got a little "peckish," as my dad always says, it would be game over for Pepper and me. But that wasn't what he meant at all.

"I've come to enlist your assistance," Simon said.

"Would you like to sit down?" I pointed at the vacant bed.

"Thank you, no. We generally stand."

A brilliant remark about circulation popped into my head, but I decided not to say it out loud.

"What kind of help?" Pepper asked.

"Ah, well, before I get into that I better explain some things about vampires to you. Some things it would be best for you to know."

We saw him move for the first time then, as he crossed the room and turned so that his back was to the wall. The thing is, he didn't walk—not really. But he didn't float either. It was as if he was in one place one minute and in another place the next, but you weren't sure how he got there. I know that sounds strange, but that's how it seemed. Pepper and I talked about it later and she thought the same thing.

"As you may know, vampires date back several hundred years, perhaps thousands. We're not sure who the first vampire was or where he or she lived, but we have been very active in the British Isles and the continent of Europe for several centuries."

"How does someone... become a vampire?" Pepper had folded her hands in her lap. I'd never seen her that calm in a crisis before.

"We are made—created, if you like—by Master Vampires. They are exactly like us except that they are often older. And they are the only ones capable of producing others."

"You mean every time one of the Master Vampires... uh... kills somebody... it makes another vampire? There must be thousands of you around."

"Wrong on three counts. First of all, the Master Vampires will create very few vampires. They look for a certain... I suppose you would call it spirit, in the living being, that would make a good vampire. There are actually very few such people in the world. You two, incidentally, would be very promising candidates."

"That's... uh... nice... to know," Pepper stammered, a little less calmly.

Simon ignored her. "Secondly, vampires do not feed nightly. Even when we are active, a feeding may last us a few days. And thirdly, there is quite a high mortality rate, particularly among newly made vampires. Mistakes are made, they lose their bearings and get caught away from their coffins when the sun comes up."

"So it's true that sunlight is fatal to vampires?" I looked at him.

"One hundred percent of the time."

"What about garlic? Does it really work or is that an old wives' tale?" Pepper had regained her composure again.

"Not fatal, but definitely a deterrent. As, by the way, is silver. That's something you may wish to remember."

"Why?" I hoped he wasn't hinting that we might be meeting more vampires.

"No particular reason. I merely make the point for your . . . interest."

I didn't like his answer and decided to change the subject. "How old are you?"

"I'm quite young really. I was made fifty-five years ago."

That really popped Pepper's eyebrows up. "But you look our age."

"That's because vampires retain the physical attributes we had at the time we were made. I was fourteen years old."

"Geez!" Pepper shook her head. "That's awful. You were murdered when you were just a kid."

"I suppose you might view it that way. But my Master, the Duke of Oronsy—who is over six hundred years old—saw that my life was going to be a very unhappy one. He felt I had the proper ingredients to be an efficient, successful vampire, so he chose me."

"You make it sound like he was doing you a favour," I said, shivering at the thought of what had happened to Simon when he was just a couple of years older than Pepper and me.

"I'm sure you would not regard it as such. Your understanding of the world does not permit it. And, indeed, a favour is perhaps the wrong idea of what happens..." He stopped and stared at the wall for a long time before speaking again.

"That brings me to what I wish to discuss with you. And to what I would like your assistance with."

"Uh-huh." I was getting kind of edgy all of a sudden. I mean, what could a vampire possibly need two teenage girls to do? Besides, the temperature in the room had been dropping ever since Simon arrived, and I was starting to shiver a lot harder.

"I understand your lack of enthusiasm, but I'm afraid I must insist that you listen to what I have to say."

"What if we decide not to help you?" I asked him.

"That is not an option."

"I was afraid of that."

He began. "About two hundred and fifty years ago, it was decided by several of the Master Vampires—among whom the Duke of Oronsy was very influential—that except in cases where a new vampire was being made, vampires would choose their victims from among the... shall we say... undesirable groups of human beings: unreformable prisoners, dangerous criminals that the authorities could not apprehend, people whose lives were destined to be dreadful and others like that. Some might even suggest that we have been performing a service for the human race—filtering out the bad blood, as it were."

I made a face. This wasn't something I wanted to hear dumb jokes about.

"We should be giving you guys medals," Pepper said sarcastically. Obviously she didn't like his sense of humour either.

Simon's shoulders moved very slightly in what I took to be a vampire shrug. I shivered again, but I don't think it had much to do with the temperature in the room. Gorgeous or not, Simon Chelling was a vampire. And a very scary guy.

"You still haven't told us what you want us to do," Pepper reminded him.

"I was just coming to that. Recently a kind of maverick gang of vampires broke away from the rest of us and its members are taking whomever they feel like taking. They refuse to adhere to the rules. They are killers, purely and simply, sometimes murdering victims for the sheer pleasure of it, and not even bothering with the blood. I assure you such behaviour is absolutely outside the vampire code of ethics. We want to stop them. But we need your help."

"You have got to be kidding," Pepper said.

"Let me get this straight." I stood up. "You've got a vampire gang war going on and you want two teenaged girls from Small Townsville to help you stop it."

"Essentially, that's correct," Simon nodded.

Pepper was shaking her head. "What... exactly... do you want from us?"

"And why us?" I added.

Simon nodded. "The answers to the two questions are related." He crossed the room again in that weird way of moving he had and stood at the window. "The renegade group has made some kind of pact with a number of humans. We're not sure, but we think the vampires receive access to secure daytime hiding places and maybe even help in obtaining victims in return for... well, that part isn't perfectly clear. But it's possible that if certain people wanted other people murdered in such a way as to leave no trace of evidence for the police, then they could strike a bargain with the outlaw vampires. You see?"

"You mean they put out a contract on someone and get a vampire to take care of it?" Pepper watches a lot of television. She knows all the cop show terminology.

The corners of Simon's eyes narrowed about half a degree. "You could put it that way if you wish, yes."

I wondered if vampires watched TV. I guessed not, since they were active only at night and were probably too busy for Letterman and all the other late-night stuff.

"That doesn't explain why you picked us," I told Simon.

He turned to look at me. His eyes were so piercing that I felt as if I didn't have control of my own thoughts. It was like being at the top of a ski hill just as you're beginning your run. There's a kind of light-headed feeling as you realize you've started down and there's no turning back. That's what it felt like when I looked at Simon—especially the "no turning back" part.

I forced myself to look away and as soon as I did, I could feel myself returning to normal. Still, there was part of me that *wanted* to look at him, to let his mind control mine. I realized the enormous power vampires had and I knew right then that the stories about vampires mesmerizing their victims weren't stories at all.

"Actually," he said, "we didn't choose you. In a way, you chose us."

I sat up straight and almost looked at him again, but I caught myself just in time.

"What do you mean?" I said.

"By coming to stay in this house you have involved yourselves whether you wanted to or not."

"I don't understand."

"We are quite certain that your host is working with the renegades. We needed someone to watch him and you very conveniently came along. Your job then will be just that: to watch him—before dark, of course. We want to know whom he sees, where he goes, who comes here, all that sort of thing."

I stood up, noticing as I did that my legs were feeling more than a little rubbery. "Well, you can forget it. In the first place, I don't believe you. Mr. Cubbington-Smith is a nice man—a gentleman—and he wouldn't be involved in *anything* like what you're describing. Even if he was, we wouldn't help you. So you can just leave us alone and—"

Simon held up his hand and even though I had lots more I wanted to say, I couldn't make my brain and my mouth work together to get the words out.

"I will return in two nights," he said in a soft, cold voice. "I will expect my first report then."

And then he was gone. Just like that. Even though I was watching, I can't tell you exactly how he left. It was the same as when he moved. He was there and then he wasn't.

I glanced at Pepper. She'd been pretty quiet for the last part of the discussion and I wanted to know if she felt the same way I did about the situation. The look on her face explained her silence: she wore a spaced-out, hypnotized sort of expression. She must have looked at Simon and then been unable to pull herself away. I went over and bent down in front of her: "Pepper . . . Pepper."

It took three more calls and some heavy-duty shoulder shaking to snap her out of it. Finally, she blinked a couple of times and looked at me.

"Are you okay?" I was still holding on to her shoulders.

"Boy, that was weird," she breathed, then blinked again and finally stood up.

I stood up, too. "I know. But vampire or not, we don't have to do what he says. What can they do to us anyway?"

"You mean besides sucking out all of our blood?" Pepper looked at me and shrugged. "Not much, I guess."

"They won't do that," I told her. "That would be against their code. We're not in any of the groups he said they feed off of." I shivered as the words came out of my mouth. It wasn't a very pleasant phrase, "feed off of."

Pepper seemed to be thinking about what I said. "Maybe, but I still don't feel real great about having vampires—even good ones—mad at me."

"Yeah, me neither."

"Chris, do you think he was telling the truth about Mr. Cubbington-Smith?"

"I doubt it," I said, but I wasn't totally sure if I doubted it or not.

"You have to admit there's some odd stuff going on here. All the garlic and everything. Maybe Mr. C. is worried about the bad vampires double-crossing him or something. And what about the locked room? The whole business is pretty strange."

"I know."

Pepper leaned forward and grabbed my arm. "Chris, I just thought of something!"

"What?"

"If Cubbington-Smith really *is* in cahoots with the renegade vampires, then they could be coming around here to see him. And there's nothing in *their* code of ethics to keep them from having us for dinner."

"True."

"Geez!"

"Okay, let's not panic here," I tried to reassure both of us at the same time.

"Right." Pepper walked over to the window and cupped her hands against the glass to look out at the black night. "Nothing to worry about. It's the vampire time of day and we're in a vampire place and we don't have any garlic on our windows. But there's no reason to panic. We'll just sit here and chill, calm as can be until we're about to become a couple of vampire sandwiches. *Then* we'll panic."

"Will you stop it!" I yelled at her. "All you're doing is scaring me to death. We have to think."

We thought. For maybe five minutes we just sat there on our beds looking at each other and thinking. We probably would have thought some more but a noise interrupted us. A kind of scratching noise.

It was coming from the direction of the fireplace. I looked at the fireplace, then at Pepper, then at the fireplace again. I noticed when I looked at Pepper that she had become very white. I figured I probably looked the same way. Which was maybe not so bad, I reasoned. Maybe we wouldn't look all that appetizing to a vampire.

On the negative side, we were about to find out. Something was about to come through the fireplace!

We Showed 'Em

We watched, frozen in place, as the back wall of the fireplace began to move. Slowly at first, then a little faster. There was a vague thought swimming around in my brain: why would a vampire spend time and energy pushing on a stone wall when it could just walk through instead? Unfortunately, that thought was lost in the waves of fear that kept rolling through my mind and over my body.

It seemed to take forever for that door to open—an eternity during which I imagined all sorts of excruciating scenarios involving Pepper, me and a host of vampires. As the wall groaned into its final open position I cringed a little and half shut my eyes, afraid of what I was about to see.

And there in the fireplace stood Hal—in his pajama bottoms, a stupid grin on his face.

"Hi," he said. "I found a secret passage. I guess this is where it comes out."

"Great," I told him as soon as I could breathe normally. "Now take yourself back down that passage and disappear."

Hal shrugged. "Sure, no problem. I'll just take this garlic with me. I found it in the kitchen and I thought I'd share with my sister and her friend, but..." He turned and started back into the passageway, pulling the wall closed behind him.

I looked at Pepper and she looked at me and though both of us hated to do it, we called after him in sweet, unisoned voices, "Hal!" The brat came back.

A look between us was all it took for Pepper and me to decide that we would keep the subject of our vampire visitor to ourselves. I knew that Hal would either (a) not believe us, (b) blab to everybody in London that his sister was madly in love with Simon Chelling (that's his favourite trick at school if I even talk to a boy) or (c) want to be there when Simon came back. I learned a long time ago that the less my brother knows about important stuff, the less chance he'll have to mess it up.

We hung garlic on the windows, the door and the ends of the beds. Pepper and Hal hung giant pieces of the stuff around their necks, but the thought of that grossed me out, so I didn't bother. Besides, I wasn't completely sure that I hadn't dreamed the whole thing. You know, sort of like Ebenezer Scrooge's visits from the ghosts. I mean this was London, after all. When I mentioned that possibility later, Pepper reminded me that, in the story, Scrooge *hadn't* dreamed the whole thing at all; it really happened. But that still didn't convince me to wear a hunk of garlic.

Hal finally padded off to his own room (the regular way—down the hall instead of through the secret passage), and Pepper and I had a chance to talk some more about what we ought to do.

"I think we'd better do what Simon told us to do," Pepper said. "In fact, if a vampire told me to bungee jump from the top of Big Ben, I'd start climbing the clock."

I shook my head. "I think our best bet is to stay out of the whole thing. I still say that Simon and his group won't take our blood. So what can he do if we refuse to spy for him? Nothing, that's what. We should keep our noses out of this whole vampire business and maybe Simon will leave us alone."

"But what if there *is* something strange about Mr. Cubbington-Smith? What if he is doing the stuff Simon said he is? You have to admit, he's pretty bizarre."

"I know he's kind of weird, all right," I nodded. "But that doesn't make him a criminal. And I don't think he's part of a gang of outlaw vampires. Think about it, Pepper. If you saw this on TV, you'd say it was a dumb show because nobody would ever believe it."

Pepper was quiet then. I guess she was thinking about what I'd said. After a while she looked at me.

"Simon is kind of cute though, isn't he?"

"Geez," I rolled my eyes. "I hope Jack the Ripper doesn't come calling. You might think he's good looking and invite him in for tea."

Pepper looked a bit worried. "Don't worry," I added. "The Ripper's been dead for about a hundred years."

"Yeah? Simon's been a corpse for more than half a century and that didn't stop *him* from showing up."

"True," I reached for my pajamas and started getting ready for bed. "So what do you say? Do we tell Simon Chelling to get lost or not?"

Pepper laid back on her bed and stared at the ceiling. She was fingering the garlic hanging around her neck.

"I guess..." she spoke slowly, which is unusual for Pepper. "I guess if you're sure it's the best idea."

"I'm positive."

Two nights later Simon showed up, just as he said he would.

"Good evening, ladies," he said in a very formal voice. He was moving around a lot more than the first time he'd visited and I assumed the garlic was making him uncomfortable.

"Good evening," I replied. Pepper didn't say anything. She just stared at a picture on the wall. I could tell she was scared.

Simon took out a notebook and pencil. "Now, what information do you have for me?"

"Nothing," I said. My voice was softer than I wanted it to be and kind of squeaky.

Simon looked up at me. "I beg your pardon?"

"Nothing. Zero. Zip. Zilch. We have no information for you."

Simon put the notebook away. "I take it then that you have decided not to assist us."

"That is correct," I nodded, avoiding eye contact with him. Pepper still hadn't moved.

"In that case, there is obviously no reason for me to prolong this visit," Simon said. I noticed that he didn't really sound angry. I guess he seemed more hurt than anything else.

"That is also correct," I said, feeling my confidence and my voice returning.

And then he was gone. Just like that. Again, I wasn't sure how he actually got out of the room, but he wasn't there any more. I looked around a couple of times to make sure that he hadn't just moved and then went and sat next to Pepper.

I tried not to let her see that I was shaking. "See?" I said, "that wasn't so hard, was it?"

"What... what if he comes back?"

"We give him the same reception. Eventually, he'll give up and leave us alone."

I could see that Pepper didn't share my optimism. "I still don't know if it's a good idea to have a vampire upset with us," she said.

"I'm telling you, it's okay." I put my hand on her shoulder. "I'll bet my entire allowance for next year that we won't be seeing any more of Simon Chelling."

"Do you really think so?"

"Of course I do." I grinned to show her there was nothing to worry about, but I had to work pretty hard to make my face do what I wanted it to.

As it turns out, Pepper was right and I was wrong. The vampires weren't about to go away.

But someone was!

Kidnapped

It was when we went down to breakfast the next morning that we discovered Hal was missing! There was no sign of him at all—odd because he's usually the first one pigging out on bacon and eggs.

A quick check of the house—nothing. Breakfast was postponed. We searched the house again and expanded our efforts to the grounds. We even visited the neighbours. When Hal still hadn't showed up by noon Mr. McKenzie phoned Scotland Yard.

Pepper and I helped with the search, but our hearts weren't in it. Both of us knew we weren't going to find Hal. He'd been taken by Simon Chelling and it was all my fault. If only I hadn't been so stubborn! But geez, I didn't want to be part of some vampire scheme! And who would have guessed Simon would go this far? Our only hope was that Hal was only a hostage—some leverage to make Pepper and me do what Simon wanted.

"What are we going to do?" Pepper wailed as we walked through one of the gardens behind the manor.

"I don't know," I told her. "I just know that Simon's kidnapped him."

"But what if they . . ." She didn't have to finish.

"There would be no point. Killing him isn't going to make us become their spies. And that's what they want. I think we'll probably see Mr. Chelling again real soon. Maybe even tonight."

Pepper sniffed. "All those things I've said about your brother, I mean I'd feel just awful if . . ."

"Me too," I said as we started back to the house. "But I don't think we should panic just yet."

"Maybe we should tell somebody."

I shook my head. "That could make things worse. If Scotland Yard and everybody else are hanging around trying to catch Simon, he might not come around. And right now, he's our best bet for getting Hal back."

"But what if Simon doesn't show up?"

"Then I guess we'll have to tell your parents. But he will. I'm positive."

"That's what you said last time."

I wished she hadn't reminded me. "Yeah, I know."

This time I was right.

Simon Chelling arrived at about ten o'clock that night.

"Good evening, ladies," he said in that strange monotone voice of his.

"No, actually it isn't." I faced him without looking at his eyes. "It isn't very good at all. And I think you know why."

"Yes, I should imagine I do. You are no doubt distressed that we found it necessary to . . . borrow your brother."

"Borrow?" I came close to yelling at him, but then I remembered I was talking to a vampire. "You kidnapped him."

"Not really," Simon shook his head. "Kidnap has a rather permanent feel to it. In this case, I merely wanted to show you that it would be best to cooperate with us."

"Is he . . . is he . . . all right?" This time, Pepper's voice was doing the squeaky thing.

"Oh, indeed," Simon floated over to the fireplace. "Of course, we did find it necessary to subdue him somewhat in order to keep him from hurting himself. All that yelling and jumping around. Quite undignified, really."

That sounded like Hal . . . undignified. "Well, we want him back." I tried to sound firm, but I wasn't sure what I'd do if Simon refused.

"I see," was all he said.

"We want him back . . . now." I was bluffing and I think all three of us knew it. After, all, how could a couple of twelve-year-old girls force a vampire to do anything it didn't want to do?

"You have reviewed my request then?"

"You mean that we become your spies?"

"You have such an unpleasant way of expressing quite reasonable concepts."

"I wouldn't call kidnapping or spying reasonable concepts," Pepper snapped at Simon. Her tone of voice surprised the heck out of him and made me kind of proud.

"I believe I explained in quite logical and legitimate terms the reason for my request. You refused. It was necessary for me to take a step I would rather not have taken. That brings us to where we are now. I repeat: you have reviewed my request?"

"When do we get Hal back?" I crossed my arms to show I meant business.

"As soon as you agree to help us."

"You mean we could have him back tonight?" That was important. Pepper's parents had naturally phoned my mom and dad and they were already trying to get a flight to England. If we could get Hal back right away, they wouldn't have to come.

"Quite so," Simon nodded.

"Where is he?"

"You agree then?"

I looked at Pepper and she looked at me, shrugging her shoulders just a little to indicate we had no choice.

"Okay," I told Simon, "we agree. Now bring Hal in here."

"I'm afraid not."

"What? You... you..." I was so mad I couldn't come up with the words I wanted.

"You promised," Pepper said.

"No," Simon started back toward the window. "What I said was that you could have him back. In fact, I am quite delighted that you should have him. I find him to be a most annoying person."

Hearing that made me feel a little better. At least there were still some things you could count on. Like my brother being annoying. "But—"

Simon held up his hand. "I did not, however, say I would deliver him. I am much too busy for that. I will tell you where he is and you may go and get him."

"Okay. Where is he?" I demanded.

"Don't be in such a hurry. First I want to make it clear that I will be back in two days at exactly this time. And I will expect a full report on the daytime comings and goings of your host. Should you refuse again, I assure you the consequences will be much more severe."

"Fine," I said. "We'll do your dirty work. Now tell us how we find Hal."

"Are you familiar with the statue of Peter Pan?"

"Yes," I replied, "we went there two days ago."

"It's in Hyde Park," Pepper added.

Simon nodded. "Correct. Directly behind the statue is a large group of trees and bushes. If you walk in a straight line from the back of Peter Pan's left heel into the bushes you will come to a set of four tree stumps cut low to the ground. They form the corners of a square. Between them, if you push away the weeds, you will find a handle. Pull on it. It will open up to a stairwell. When you reach the bottom of the stairs, turn right. You will be in a tunnel. Walk seventy-five paces and turn right again. Thirty more paces and you will find a door. Unlock the door. Your detestable little brother will be behind that door. I must warn you: there are many tunnels and they are very dark. It is best not to become lost. You may never get back. Remember seventy-five paces, then thirty."

I nodded. "What about the key to the door?"

Simon reached into his pocket and took out a long old brass key. He laid it on the edge of the bed.

"What about...?" I never finished the question and it wouldn't have mattered anyway. He was gone.

I sat down on the edge of the bed staring at the key. I wanted to cry. The last thing I needed in my life was a trip into underground London—dark, scary underground London. I looked at Pepper. She seemed pretty calm.

"You know, for a cute guy, that Simon is such a loser," she said.

I'm not a good sneaker-outer. In fact, the only time I ever tried was when Pepper and I wanted to see this really gross slasher movie and my mom told me I couldn't go. I made it out of the house and was pretty proud of myself... right up until Pepper and I arrived at the box office—just in time to see my mom and dad park the car right in front of the theatre. They didn't say a word. They just bought tickets and sat right behind us. I never enjoyed a movie less. And I never snuck out of the house again.

This time, I left the planning to Pepper. Turns out she's a lot better at it than me. She arranged for a restaurant delivery of fish and chips (enough for ten people!) to arrive just minutes before our planned departure. While Pepper's mom and dad were outside arguing with the delivery guy, we started our sneak.

There was a lot of manor to get through. And every time we turned a corner I was convinced we'd run right into Mr. and Mrs. McKenzie...and their fish and chips. Finally we were down to the last corner; then we'd be home free to one of the side doors. I guess we got a little overconfident. We turned the corner and ran smack into Mrs. Pudkins. Standing in front of us, she looked quite a bit scarier than most of the characters in the slasher movie. She didn't say anything, she just crept closer and closer. Then, just as Pepper and I were holding our breath, she burst out laughing. Except it was a laugh that you'd expect to hear from a hysterical chicken. And I noticed that Mrs. Pudkins did not have nice teeth.

She didn't say anything. She just laughed some more, then rushed off to the front of the house. We watched her through one of the manor's giant windows. We were sure she was going to squeal on us, but she didn't. She just grabbed some of the fish and chips and scurried back into the house—still giggling. The whole thing was getting weirder all the time. But Mrs. Pudkins did provide an excellent diversion and we made it out of the manor without further excitement.

We took the Tube—which is what Londoners call their subway—into the main part of the city. Our destination was Paddington Station. As a kid, I'd read all about the place and the bear that belonged there. Still, I didn't enjoy the trip. Not one little bit.

I couldn't help it. I kept going over what Simon had said about getting lost. I had this picture in my head of Pepper and me stumbling around in the dark until we finally died of hunger. No one would ever know what happened to us.

The only thing that kept me from panicking completely was Pepper's chattering, something she did for the entire ride. I could tell she was looking at the whole thing as an adventure, which Pepper usually is crazy about. Except, of course, for face-to-face meetings with vampires.

"Imagine!" she said. "We're going into underground London! This is going to be so cool."

"Yeah, cool," I said, not very enthusiastically. "But you know what's bothering me, Pepper?"

"What?"

"Well, how did those tunnels get there? It's not like Rome where they have catacombs that were built hundreds of years ago. By people. London doesn't have catacombs.

What if these tunnels are where the vampires live? What if they built them? What if they're down there right now? What if—"

"Hold it." Pepper grabbed my arm. "If you keep that up, you'll be going down there alone. Besides, you said yourself that the vampires wouldn't want us because it's against their bylaws."

"Ethics," I corrected. "Besides, I was talking about Simon's vampires. What if the *other* vampires live in the tunnels? The bad ones?"

Pepper didn't say any more after that and we were both pretty quiet for the rest of the trip. The question that kept popping into my brain was, "How much do I love my brother?"

An Underground Search

We got off the train at Paddington Station and walked along Eastbourne Terrace to the edge of Hyde Park. But we didn't go into the park right away. We both needed a little time to work up our courage. We walked along the outer edge of the park past Marble Arch, where we turned and walked some more until we came to Speakers' Corner. It's this cool place where anybody can stand up and make a speech about anything. Some guy was going on about how Prime Minister Tony Blair and Mick Jagger from The Rolling Stones were actually twins and how Mick was making all the decisions for his brother. I guess you don't have to be totally, like, sane to make a speech at Speakers' Corner.

We left there after a while and turned onto a path that would take us into the park. We crossed over the Serpentine—a huge lake in the middle of the park—and finally came to the statue of Peter Pan.

I looked around. Nobody was in the park. No lovebirds, no old people—there had been lots of both when we'd visited in the daytime. Now, the place was deserted.

"Well, I guess this is it." I looked at the bushes and trees behind the statue. It was like a mini-forest. There wasn't a path or even an opening.

Pepper pointed. "His left heel points off in that direction."

"Terrific," I said. But I didn't feel terrific.

We pushed aside branches and leaves, but in the darkness we couldn't see a thing. And, naturally, we'd forgotten to bring the one thing we could have used—a flashlight.

"We'll have to feel our way along."

I nodded, which was stupid, come to think of it, since a scary thought entered my mind: Pepper couldn't see me in the dark. For once, I was actually glad she was in a talkative mood. At least I could keep track of where she was. If it was this dark above-ground, what would it be like in the tunnels below?

"I remember this part of the park from when we were here before." Pepper was chatting away like we were on a picnic. "It was very pretty. All sorts of wildflowers. Columbine, I think, and some lovely little yellow ones—oof!"

From the "oof" and the crashing sound that followed, I guessed that Pepper must have fallen down.

"Are you okay?" I whispered. I don't know why I was

whispering, except that it was nighttime and we were sort of sneaking around. Anyway, I whispered.

"Yeah, I'm fine," Pepper said in her normal voice. "Tripped over a root."

"I wonder if we'll ever find those stumps."

I could hear brushing sounds. Pepper must have been cleaning herself off. "Of course we will," she said. "It can't be much farther."

The longer we looked, the madder I got at Simon Chelling for not bringing Hal back. Too busy, he had said. He wasn't too busy to kidnap him in the first place, was he?

We pushed our way through more brush and a branch smacked me in the face. My mood was not improving.

Pepper giggled. I couldn't believe it. Here we were in the darkest part of Hyde Park, in the darkest part of the night, about to go down into the darkest part of the whole world ... and she was giggling.

"What's so funny?"

"I was just thinking. Here we are at Peter Pan's statue. We could sure use a little help from Tinker Bell right now."

I didn't even bother to answer. Sometimes Pepper's sense of humour is pretty dumb. Besides, I was sure she was just putting on an act so I wouldn't know how scared she really was.

She giggled again and then suddenly stopped. "Chris," she hissed. "I think I've found it. Over here."

I stumbled over to where I thought her voice was coming from. I had to crouch to keep from being hit in the face by more branches. Finally my hand came in contact with what felt like a human leg. I hoped it was Pepper's.

"Can you find the handle?" I whispered.

"Sure, I'll just feel my way around until... here. It's right here, Chris."

That's when I noticed that it wasn't completely dark any more. There was the tiniest amount of light coming from somewhere. It wasn't enough light to actually let us see anything. But it was light just the same and it made me feel a little better.

"You'd better take my hand," I told Pepper. "If we get separated now, we might never find each other again."

We held hands and slowly pulled on the handle. Simon hadn't bothered to mention that the cover was heavy. Real heavy. It made a little creaking sound, but in the quiet of the park's noiseless night, it sounded like a scream.

Pepper snickered. I was beginning to get a little irritated. "What is it this time?"

"I wonder if Simon did it on purpose." She was talking loudly again.

"Did what?"

"Well, you remember in *Peter Pan* the kids in Never Never Land were called the Lost Boys? Well, here we are by the statue of Peter Pan looking for a lost boy."

"You know, you think of the stupidest things at the stupidest times," I told her as we started down. We struggled to get the cover back in place behind us. "Let's take it slow going down these steps."

The light I'd seen before was coming from somewhere down below, but there wasn't enough of it for us to actually see the stairs. We had to feel with our feet to get down. It took a long time, but at least Pepper didn't think of anything else totally useless to say. When we got to the bottom we could see that the light was coming from a lantern on the wall at the entrance to the passageway. Unfortunately, it had about as much power as a candle and obviously wouldn't be much help once we were in the tunnel.

"Okay," I said. "Remember, we turn right, and then it's seventy-five paces until we turn again."

"Uh-huh."

"Ready?"

"I guess so." Now that we were actually about to enter the long, black tunnel, Pepper's courage seemed to be disappearing.

We held hands again and counted in unison. By the time we reached twenty, the light had given out. We were in complete darkness. At thirty-seven, Pepper stopped.

I thought maybe she'd heard something. "What's wrong?"

"What if our steps aren't the right size?" She was also whispering now. "He didn't tell us what size of paces, did he? I mean if they're the wrong size, we could miss the next tunnel."

"I'm sure he meant average size," I assured her. "And ours are about average. Now come on."

When we started again, I said, "Thirty-eight." Pepper said, "Thirty-four."

"Thirty-eight," I corrected.

"Thirty-four," she argued.

"It's thirty-eight."

"It's thirty-four."

I was getting more and more scared and more and more grumpy. "Fine. Let go of my hand and you start counting at thirty-four and I'll start at thirty-eight and maybe we'll meet up somewhere down there."

"I think it's thirty-eight, after all," Pepper said very softly.

"Fine. Come on."

We resumed counting and after what seemed like an hour we got to seventy-five.

"We're here," I said, not at all sure where exactly "here" was.

"Right." Pepper sounded out of breath. I'm sure it wasn't from strenuous exercise—we'd been walking at the speed of ants moving through molasses—so I figured it was because she was terrified. I felt the same way, but I was trying not to show it.

"Okay, now we turn right," I said, careful not to let go of her hand.

We turned right, took a couple of steps and ran smack into a damp and very hard wall.

I stepped back holding my nose and wondered if it was bleeding. I had a feeling, though I couldn't tell for sure in the dark, that Pepper was probably doing the same thing.

"There's no opening there."

"No kidding," I said. "The last thing I need to hear right at this minute is the obvious."

"What do we do, Chris?"

I could hear panic rising in Pepper's voice. I had no idea what I was going to do if she freaked in a black tunnel under London. I knew I had to calm her down, so I tried to sound like I was in control.

"Okay, we must have been out a little bit," I said, which, come to think of it, was also kind of on the obvious side. "So I'll just feel my way to the right and you feel your way to the left until one of us comes to the opening."

"Can we do that and still hold onto each other's hand?"

"I'm afraid not."

"Then I don't want to do that."

"We have to," I told her.

"No, we don't. We can both go to the right and if we don't find it that way then we can both go left. That way we stay together."

I figured I better not push her. To tell the truth, I was just as happy not to let go of her right at that moment myself.

We started inching our way along the wall. It felt kind

of gross, like we were running our hands over slime and bugs and who knows what else.

"It can't be far," I said, mostly to boost our confidence. To be honest, I had no idea where the opening was.

My hand hit something soft—well, not really soft, but softer than the wall. I wasn't sure that was a good sign. What I really wanted to feel was nothing, which would have meant we were at the opening to the next tunnel. I felt around a little to try to figure out what it was.

"This is weird, Pepper," I whispered. "It feels like a—"

"Hello," said a voice.

Two for the Price of One?

Now I've never actually died before so I can't say for sure what it's like, but I think when I heard that voice in the tunnel and realized that what I'd been touching was a face, I came awfully close to finding out what being dead is all about.

My heart skipped at least three beats, and when I finally got my voice to work, I did the only thing that seemed to make sense.

I screamed.

I screamed as loud as I have ever screamed in my life.

Then Pepper screamed.

Then I screamed and then she screamed and then we screamed together.

Because it had been so quiet in the tunnel up until that moment, our screaming seemed even louder than normal, which scared us again, and we screamed some more.

The voice didn't say anything. No soothing, feel better little phrases. No "Now, now, nothing to worry about, I'm sorry I startled you." Nothing.

So Pepper and I went on screaming until we got tired. Then it took us quite a while to get our breath back. Finally I was able to croak out a few words. "Who . . . are . . . you?"

"My name is Leonard Livermore," the voice answered.

Not Leonard Jones, or Leonard Brown, or even Leonard Khalmikov. Instead, we meet up with somebody—in the total blackness of that tunnel, remember—with an internal organ as part of his name.

"Are you a . . ."

"Vampire? Oh yes, yes, indeed," the voice chuckled. Who else would be down here? it seemed to ask.

"Whose . . . side . . . are you on?" I said this very slowly knowing full well that the voice's answer would tell us how much longer we could expect to go on living.

"Side?" He seemed puzzled.

"Yes, you know. Are you with Simon Chelling and his group or . . ."

"Ah, Simon," the voice chuckled again. "He *is* a rascal, isn't he?"

"He sure is." I thought I should chuckle too. "A real rascal, that Simon."

"Would you like me to light a lantern?"

"Oh, could you, Mr. Livermore?" It was the first time Pepper had spoken since we'd stopped screaming. It was a bit of a relief to hear her voice. I had begun to wonder if she'd fainted.

There was a scratching sound and the flare of a match. Once the flame steadied, Leonard lit the lantern. The light was welcome after what had seemed like hours in the dark.

As my eyes adjusted, I stared at the person in front of us—except of course he wasn't a person. He was a vampire, maybe the oldest vampire on the planet. Leonard must have been *ancient* when he was created.

Pepper must have been thinking the same thing. "You're quite... aged," she said, which I thought was kind of rude.

"Yes, I am." Leonard was different from Simon Chelling in a lot of ways. The age was the obvious thing, but he also smiled quite often and even laughed sometimes. Still, he did have that same pale, bloodless skin. The good thing was the white skin was the *only* thing even remotely scary about Leonard.

He laughed now, and his slightly bent-over body bent over a little more. "I was one hundred and three," he said quite proudly. "That's the oldest a vampire has ever been created. And that was in 1761 when people didn't live as long as they do today."

"You mean... you were alive two hundred and fifty years ago?"

"My dear girl," Leonard chuckled, "two hundred and fifty years ago, I was already ninety-seven years old. I had been in prison for forty-seven years at that time."

"Prison?" I shuddered and looked at Pepper and then back at Leonard. "What for?"

"Murder."

I swallowed. Pepper's hand, which was still in mine, suddenly felt a lot colder.

Leonard's posture improved slightly. In fact, he almost straightened up completely. He seemed quite upset all of a sudden and his voice became much louder. "I spent the last sixty-six years of my life imprisoned for a murder I did not commit!"

Seeing him that angry made me nervous. "I... I'm sorry, Mr. Livermore," I said.

He seemed to calm down then. "Sorry?" he said. "Why should you be sorry? You didn't have anything to do with it." He chuckled then, as if he'd made a joke.

"Yes, I know, but I just thought... I mean, I feel bad that something like that happened to you."

"Me too," Pepper nodded.

"Ah, well, thank you," he leaned toward us and lowered his voice to a whisper, "but I'm planning my revenge."

"Excuse me?" I said.

"Certain people lied in order to have me sent to prison, but..." he tapped his forehead, "revenge will be mine."

Not only were we talking to an old vampire, we were talking to a senile vampire. "But isn't that kind of impossible?" I asked. "I mean, aren't the people who lied and framed you..."

"Dead?"

"Uh... yeah," I nodded.

"Oh yes," Leonard chuckled. "Jaglers is dead to begin with... as a doornail..." He stopped then and I thought it might be a good idea to change the subject.

"Do you think you could help us, Leonard?"

"I don't know. That depends on what you need help with." The lantern began to flicker and he fidgeted with the wick a little to keep it going.

"We're trying to find my brother."

Leonard laughed out loud then, so suddenly and so loudly that both Pepper and I took a step backward.

"You mean that unruly little man is your brother?"

"Well, I do have a brother who is... unruly, all right, and he was brought here by Simon and we were sent to get him back, but we can't find him." I took a breath.

"Well then, I certainly *can* help you," Leonard turned slowly. "Indeed, it will be my pleasure to do so. Come with me."

He led us farther into the tunnel. A lot farther.

"This is a heck of a lot more than seventy-five paces," I whispered to Pepper. "Simon must have been trying to get us lost in here."

Leonard obviously had exceptional hearing. "He's quite a joker, that Simon. Always playing tricks on people."

"Yeah, he's a million laughs, all right," I muttered.

Finally we made a right turn into a passage that was narrower and lower than the one we were in. We almost had to duck our heads.

"I'm getting claustrophobia," Pepper said. "How much farther is it?"

"Not far," Leonard said without turning around.

I was beginning to feel a little panicky myself. Even if we weren't lost, the situation was pretty bleak: two teenaged (well, almost) girls following a vampire senior citizen down a very small tunnel, a long way under the streets of London. The kids back at school would never believe this one. Not that it mattered, since it was unlikely we'd live long enough to tell them.

"Here we are," Leonard said at last. I looked around, but I couldn't see anything different. That part of the tunnel seemed just like the rest, except that it was even more damp. The air was thicker too, making it kind of hard to breath.

"Where's the door?" Pepper asked.

"There." Leonard pointed at a section of the tunnel wall that didn't look at all like a door.

"Are you sure?" I thought maybe he was putting us on. Being a joker like Simon. Just what we needed, a couple of vampire comedians.

Leonard leaned forward and pushed aside a clump of something that looked like moss. "Do you have the key?"

"Oh, the key." I'd almost forgotten. I was too busy thinking about the fact that vampires seem very big on hiding things. I fished in my pocket, found the key and handed it to him. "Right here."

I got closer to where he'd pushed the moss stuff away. Sure enough, there was a keyhole there.

"We would never have found this," I said.

"Probably not," Leonard chortled, no doubt thinking about what a wild and crazy guy Simon was.

The instant the key made its first little clanking noise in the metal keyhole, the tunnel was filled with noise. Familiar noise. Little brother noise.

"Open the door you dork-brained slime-faced puke bag!"

There was no doubt about it. We'd found Hal. And I'll give him credit. He obviously wasn't a coward. A coward would not direct his most disgusting vocabulary at his captors. Especially these captors.

Leonard swung the door open. Hal and Leonard stared at each other.

"Do you speak like that to your parents?" Leonard peered at Hal. "I'll wager you don't dare."

"Yeah, well, they've never locked me up in a tunnel." Hal stared back at the old vampire.

"Perhaps they should consider it. You can be a most unpleasant young chap." Leonard's mouth wrinkled at the corners as he said it.

"Yeah? Well, you're no prize yourself, puss-butt."

Hal hadn't seen Pepper and me yet. I stepped into the light and smiled, hoping to distract him before he said something he might regret.

"It's about time you showed up!" My brother has never been good with greetings.

At least I knew we'd rescued the right little brother. For a minute I thought about turning around and leaving him there for a few more days, but I knew I never wanted to come down into the tunnels again.

"And get me out of this stupid thing!" Hal hollered, as he tried to take a step toward us. That's when I realized there was a shackle around his leg. He was chained to the wall.

"Whose idea was it to chain him up?" I turned on Leonard.

"Not mine, I assure you," he shook his head apologetically.

"No doubt it was Simon," Pepper sounded as mad as I was. "Boy, that guy's a real jerk."

"Oh, great," Hal said as he saw Pepper for the first time. "Now all the rocket scientists are here."

"If I release you, will you behave yourself?" Leonard took a step back from Hal.

It was sort of comical to watch a vampire who seemed almost afraid of my little brother. On the other hand, Leonard *was* a vampire. If Hal made him mad enough, he might decide to have a little late-night snack.

"He'll behave," I told Leonard.

"Oh yeah? When I get out of this—"

"Hal, shut up!" I said in my best older sister voice.

Hal doesn't usually pay any attention to me, no matter what voice I use. That's why I was totally surprised when he actually shut up. Even after Leonard unlocked the chain, Hal just rubbed his leg and gave all of us dirty looks.

I bent down to look at Hal's leg. It was rubbed kind of raw where the metal collar had been, but otherwise he looked okay.

"Can you walk all right?"

"Of course I can walk all right. I can do cartwheels if it'll get me out of this dump."

I looked at Leonard. "I'm not sure we can find..."

"I will show you the way out," Leonard nodded and shuffled off down the tunnel. We made a point of not getting too far behind. Even Hal, sore leg and all, managed to keep up.

After a couple of minutes I realized we weren't going back the same way we'd come. For one thing, we had taken three turns already—one more than we'd made getting to Hal's cell.

"Are you sure this is the way?" I asked Leonard, not wanting to be pushy.

"Shortcut," was all he said.

We made another turn not long after that and Hal, Pepper and I stopped cold. In front of us was the scariest sight I'd ever seen. My legs have never felt more like whipped cream than they did right then. Lined up on both sides of the tunnel were coffins that stretched as far down the tunnel as we could see. A lot of the lids were open.

Leonard must have realized that we'd stopped. He turned back to us. "Well, are you coming?"

"Uh... is this really the best way out?" I asked him.

"We don't really mind going the long way," Pepper added.

"Come along." Leonard's mouth turned up at the corners again. "It isn't much farther."

As we walked by the open coffins we couldn't help looking in.

"Some of them don't make their beds," Leonard chuckled.

"You mean... this is where the... vampires... sleep?" Leonard seemed to be enjoying the fact that we were totally freaked.

"Of course! That's why these tunnels were built a couple of centuries ago. At times it was just too difficult to get back to our hiding places before daylight. This is what you might call a vampire apartment."

I looked at Pepper and she looked at me. So it *was* the vampires who built the tunnels.

"Except there's only basement suites," Hal said. Trust him to say something totally dumb. Leonard, however, seemed to enjoy Hal's sense of humour. Come to think of it, they were sort of alike that way.

There was barely room for us to get between the two rows of coffins, even walking single file. Finally, after one more turn, we were at the bottom of a set of steps, not the same ones we'd come down.

Leonard pointed. "When you reach the top of the stairs there will be a grate. Not heavy. Push it away and climb out. Then walk straight ahead through the bushes. Don't forget to return the grate to where it belongs. You'll be on the other side of the Serpentine." Leonard turned and began shuffling back down the tunnel. He seemed sort of edgy all of a sudden and I wondered why. It was like he was in a hurry to get rid of us. Then I remembered that he was, after all, a vampire. Maybe he was feeling the need for blood, and here we were—three humans, just full of the stuff. Maybe he was getting away from us because of the temptation. Sort of like me when a second piece of my mom's double chocolate cake was sitting in front of me.

"Goodbye, Leonard," I called to him.

"And thank you," Pepper added.

Leonard didn't answer, but we could hear the rustling of his footsteps as he disappeared back into the tunnel.

"Maggot," Hal muttered under his breath, but I don't think Leonard heard him.

I turned to Hal. "Without him we never would have found you." I wanted to say more to my ungrateful little creep of a brother, but the light was disappearing as Leonard's bent form scuttled farther into the tunnel. I figured we'd better get up the stairs.

We started up quickly and easily found the opening to the surface. That's because Hal charged on ahead and smacked his head into the bars of the grate. I was going to tell him he deserved it, but the kid had had a pretty rough twenty-four hours, so I just pushed the grate out of the way. All three of us climbed out into the night's welcome air.

We had a little trouble getting the grate back where it belonged, but we felt around in the dark until we finally heard it clank into place. When we got through the bushes and out where we could see stars and city lights, each of us took several deep breaths. I don't know about Hal and Pepper, but mine were definitely sighs of relief.

On the way home we talked about the tunnels.

"Two hundred years they've been living down there," Pepper breathed.

"Well, during the day at least," I said.

"It's amazing no one else has ever found the tunnels," Pepper said. "I mean that entrance behind Peter Pan's statue wouldn't be impossible to stumble across. Or this one either."

"Maybe people *have* found the tunnels," Hal shrugged, "but once they're down there, they'd never find their way out. Then, when the vampires come back . . . it would be too late."

It was a horrible thought, but the worst part of it was that Hal could be right. None of us said anything for a while.

Nobody felt much like travelling on anything that went underground and, thankfully, we had enough money for a cab. We sat in the back watching some of London's most famous landmarks passing by. They looked very different at night.

"Well," Hal looked at Pepper and me, "when are you

going to tell me what's going on?"

For a while now, a disturbing thought had been circulating in the back of my mind: the worst part of Simon's scheme to kidnap Hal was that my bigmouth brother would have to be told the whole story. It looked like the time had come.

Pepper and I exchanged looks and a little nod. Between us we told Hal everything about Simon's visit. We spoke in whispers because we didn't want the driver to overhear us.

"So what do we do now?" Pepper asked when we'd finished.

"Simple," Hal grinned. "We become spies for the vampires." He made it sound like some fun-filled adventure.

"I'm afraid he's right," I told Pepper. "I don't see what choice we have. There's no telling what else Simon might do if we don't cooperate."

We all sat in silence for a couple of minutes sorting out our own thoughts.

"I wonder what Cubbington-Smith is up to," Hal said suddenly.

"We don't know that he's up to anything," I answered.

"Oh yeah?" Hal pointed at the street. "Then why is he sneaking around in the middle of the night?"

Sure enough, a man was scurrying along the sidewalk. He was wearing a cloak and a hood and his hand was raised as if to keep passersby from seeing his face. He was looking from side to side very nervously, and as he turned to look in our direction, the hood fell away. I could clearly see the man's face.

Hal was right. The man hurrying along a London street in the middle of the night was our host, Mr. Peter Cubbington-Smith!

Spying 101

We scrunched down in the taxi so he wouldn't see us, but I don't think it would have mattered. He probably didn't even see the taxi. His face was twisted with fear and... I don't know, something else too. We peeked over the back seat and watched for as long as we could.

"How far are we from the manor?" Pepper was whispering, as if she wanted to make sure the strange figure on the street wouldn't hear her.

"I don't think it's very far," I found myself whispering, too. "He must be on his way home."

Before I could stop him, Hal leaned forward and yelled at the driver to stop the taxi.

"What are you doing?" I grabbed Hal's arm.

"We're going to follow him. That's what we're supposed to be doing, isn't it?" Hal jumped out of the cab so fast I lost my hold on him. "Don't forget to pay the man," he grinned at me over his shoulder.

I wasn't in the mood to lose my brother only an hour after I'd found him. I had no choice but to pay the cabbie. Pepper and I took to the street after that.

"Some people actually sleep at night," I reminded Hal when we caught up to him.

"Yeah, and some people don't bother with rescuing twerps from tunnels or following English gentlemen around the streets of London at three in the morning," Pepper added, but I noticed she was smiling as she dodged behind a bush with Hal.

"He's going to come right by here," Hal hissed at me, "so it might be a good idea if you were to hide."

He had a point. I joined them behind the bush and the three of us crouched down to wait for the arrival of Mr. Cubbington-Smith.

"We're only supposed to be *daytime* spies," I reminded Pepper and Hal. "Simon said the vampires would watch him at night. Maybe they're watching him, and us, right now." I noticed neither of them was paying any attention to what I was saying.

I also noticed, rather unhappily, that our taxi had driven off. There was no turning back now. That wasn't good because if there's one thing I've learned in my twelve—almost thirteen—years on the earth it's that most of my brother's ideas turn out to be disasters. I was pretty sure this one would be no different, but there was no more time to discuss it. We could hear footsteps coming along the sidewalk.

I got as low to the ground as I could and crossed all the fingers and toes I could cross without hurting myself. I could see Mr. Cubbington-Smith through the branches of whatever kind of bush we were hiding behind. He was passing below a street lamp and there was no doubt about it. This was no ordinary evening walk. He was worried about something and was spending a fair amount of time looking behind him.

As far as I could see, no one was following him. He went by our hiding place without seeing us, which was a major relief. When he was out of sight, Hal started after him, but this time I was able to grab him before he could get far.

"That's enough for one night, Sherlock." I tightened my grip on his shirt. "We're going home to bed."

"But we should follow him."

Pepper shook her head. "I think Chris is right. I've had all the excitement I can stand for one night."

I was glad she agreed with me. You just never know with Pepper.

"You two are suppressing evidence," Hal accused us.

Any time Hal says something that sounds even slightly intelligent, it usually means he's repeating something he's heard on TV. I doubt if my brother has a clue what "suppressing evidence" actually means. In fact, the only subjects my brother is capable of discussing are the ones that usually appeal to dorky ten-year-old boys. Stuff like hockey, skateboards, Arnold Schwarzenegger movies—you know the kind of thing.

"You two are accessories to a crime," Hal rattled on.

"You've been watching *Law & Order* again, haven't you?" I glared at him. "Listen, Hal, we are going home right now. No more spying. No more sneaking around." I took hold of his ear and yanked.

"Leggo," he twisted his head around, "or I'll yell so loud I'll bring every London bobby for fifteen miles."

I was beginning to sympathize with Leonard Livermore. I let go and we started back toward the manor. Maybe Hal was getting tired (I know I was) or maybe he was just crabby, but he was quiet for the rest of the walk home.

Just before we got back, I realized we still had one problem left to solve. I turned to Pepper. "How are we going to explain where he's been and why we're all arriving back here in the middle of the night?"

She just shrugged. "I don't know. I can't think any more. I just want to go to bed."

"I know. Me, too. But we can't just march in there like we were out for a walk and happened to stumble across Hal strolling through Hyde Park. And I don't think your parents are quite ready for the truth."

"We could tell them Hal ran away and then changed his mind. And he woke us up to—"

"No way," Hal suddenly became interested in the conversation. "I'm not getting into trouble for something that wasn't my fault. As a matter of fact, you two are to blame. If anyone should get into—"

"Nobody's going to get into trouble," I told him. "But we have to tell them something. And it can't be anything to do with vampires."

"How about we just say that Hal wasn't feeling good last night and he went for a walk to get some fresh air. He got lost and then he fell asleep and slept through the whole day because he was so sick, but then he woke up and found his way home and we were sitting by our window sick with worry when we saw him walking forlornly along and..."

I held my hand up to stop her. "I get the picture." I was afraid she'd go on until morning. "It isn't great, but it's the only story we've got." I didn't tell her it wouldn't have much of a chance in the believability department if *she* told it.

It didn't matter, as it turned out. We stepped inside through the same door we'd gone out of hours before—we'd deliberately left it unlocked when we went out, and the place was completely quiet. I was kind of surprised that nobody was around, but I guess even with all the worry and everything, they had to get some sleep.

We went into one of the rooms on the main floor—a big library-looking room with a jillion books in it—and called Mom and Dad. They were really glad we called because they were booked on a plane three hours later. They talked to Hal and I have to admit my brother did a good job of calming everybody down. By the end of the conversation, Dad said they'd cancel their flight and see us when we got home. Of course there was a "you three look after yourselves" warning before Dad hung up.

We left the study and were tiptoeing upstairs when Hal grabbed my arm and pointed. I looked up just in time to see someone coming out of the room next to ours—the room that Mrs. Pudkins said nobody ever used. The person didn't look around and it's a good thing because he would have seen us for sure. He closed the door, locked it very carefully and hurried off down the hall.

Pepper, Hal and I exchanged looks. At least we were going to have a few things to report when Simon Chelling dropped around again. The person sneaking out of the mystery room was Peter Cubbington-Smith!

12

High-Level Sneaking

Breakfast the next morning was a mixture of emotions. The McKenzies were overjoyed to have Hal back and pleased that we'd phoned Mom and Dad. That seemed to outweigh the suspicious looks they kept throwing at the three of us. Naturally, there were plenty of questions, first from Mr. and Mrs. McKenzie, then from two Scotland Yard detectives. We had decided to go with the "little boy lost" story and Hal pulled it off, surprising me for the second time in less than twelve hours.

I was glad when breakfast was finally over. Before they left, the police gave us all warnings about getting lost in a strange city. Then, Mr. and Mrs. McKenzie went off to have their coffee outside on the lawn with Mr. Cubbington-Smith who had just come downstairs looking a little tired but otherwise normal. As normal as someone can look with a giant hunk of garlic around his neck. I decided to polish off one more piece of cold, dry toast—just one more thing about the English that I'd never understand.

"We've got to get into that room," Hal said, looking around to make sure no one was listening.

Pepper nodded and I swallowed.

"What?" I said. "What room?"

"Hello? The *secret* room." Hal rolled his eyes like I was stupid. "We've got to get in there."

"What for?" I looked at them.

"There's obviously something important about that room." Hal spoke slowly like he was talking to a little kid. "We need to know everything we can to solve whatever's going on around here."

"We're not trying to *solve* anything," I reminded him.

"It's our duty," he announced and Pepper nodded again, which really bugged me. "Besides we're supposed to report on everything to Simon—and that includes whatever's in that room."

"He's right," Pepper said.

"No, he isn't." I set my toast down and looked at both of them. "You two are forgetting that Simon Chelling can go anywhere he wants at any time. Locked doors don't seem to be a big problem for him. He can probably tell *us* what's in there."

Hal thought about that for a minute. It was hard to tell from the look on Pepper's face what she was thinking.

"You're right," Hal said finally. "When he comes around for his report, we'll ask him."

"Wrong," I said.

"Why?" Pepper asked. "It seems like a pretty good idea to me."

"See?" Hal smiled at Pepper. He smiles at people only when they agree with him. Or when he wants something.

"Uh-uh," I shook my head. "Haven't you ever heard what happens to people when they know too much?" I decided to use an argument they could both relate to—television. "You hear that all the time on TV. 'She knows too much, we'll have to eliminate her.' Right?"

It worked, sort of.

"Yeah, okay," Hal nodded. "But there's a difference between knowing too much and not knowing enough. We have to go in there so that we know as much about what's going on around here as possible. It's for our own protection."

There was Pepper with the nod again.

"See, it's two against one," Hal grinned at me. "We move in tonight."

He made it sound like an action movie. The only problem was Vin Diesel wouldn't be there. Just two twelve-year-old girls and one pain-in-the-butt brother. I was beginning to long for a normal night. You know the kind: a good book, a bowl of popcorn, regular sleep, maybe a dream or two. This trip to England was becoming stranger every day.

Hal was really getting into this spying business. He was very pleased with himself when he showed up at our room about nine o'clock that night with the news that a yew tree (he didn't know the name of the tree—I found that out later) stood outside our window. He said it was the answer to our problem. The reason it was the answer to our problem, Hal figured, was that if certain people were to work their way along the branches, a small jump would put certain people on the balcony outside the "mystery room."

I went outside to check. Even in the semi-dark I could tell that the "small jump" was exactly the kind that could cause certain people to break certain parts of their bodies if they happened to miss the balcony. Which, by the way, looked like a pretty good possibility to me.

The vote turned out to be two to one again. I was getting a little tired of this. Fifteen minutes later I found myself a very long way off the ground on a branch that creaked and croaked under the weight of three *certain people.*

Hal was in the lead. Pepper was next and I was last. I figured this was both good and bad. Good because if one of the others chickened out, I wouldn't have to make the jump. And bad because if they didn't chicken out . . . I didn't like to think about that part, but I knew it was bad.

I'm not what you would call athletic. I like to ride my horse in horse shows and gymkhanas. And I like to read. I don't like to pitch, hit, shoot, punt, pass or jump. Especially jump. Which is why I didn't like thinking about how I'd get from the tree to the balcony.

Hal made the jump easily. I hated him. I mean even more than usual. I didn't want him to fall, but he could have at least made it look harder. Which might have scared Pepper off. And given me an out.

Didn't happen. Pepper went next and although her flight was noisier than Hal's, it was just as successful. Which meant that their two faces were over there, safely on the balcony, looking back at me and silently urging me to kill myself. Because I was pretty sure that's what would happen once I left the yew tree and leaped across a space that might as well have been the Grand Canyon.

"Why don't you two go in and check it out and I'll stand guard out here in case somebody comes along," I said in a loud stage whisper.

"That's stupid, Chris." Pepper made a face at me. "Who's going to be coming along through the branches of a tree?"

"Oh, you'd be surprised how many English people spend their evenings climbing trees," Hal said, sarcastically. "That's how Tarzan got his start."

"Come on," Pepper waved me over.

I figured there was no point in delaying the thing any longer, although I would have liked to have written my will before I jumped. But there wasn't time, so I counted to three, took a breath and jumped.

Afterward, Pepper said she really admired me for not screaming even once on my way to the ground.

Down for the Count

The thing about collarbones is that you don't really notice them until you break one. Then it seems that they're in the way all of the time.

I found that out a few minutes after I woke up on a very hard piece of ground under the yew tree. I don't know if the fall knocked me out or if I fainted on the way down. All I know is that when I woke up, the first face I saw was Hal's, a lot closer to mine than I like it to be. He was very excited and whispering at me.

"It's okay, Chris. I got in the room. A very weird place, no kidding. And don't worry, Pepper and I have a perfect story figured out for how you..."

That's all I remember because just then it felt like a heavy curtain—the kind you see in old movie theatres, except this one was black—slowly covered my face. I went to sleep again.

The next time I woke up, Hal's face was gone and a bunch of others had taken its place. Doctors' and nurses' faces. That's when I figured out that I must have hurt myself in the fall. They were throwing around the hospital vocabulary quite a bit too. *Compound fracture*, *concussion*, *contusions* and some other stuff that I didn't understand. I wished that I'd spent as much time with *ER* as Hal had with *Law & Order*.

I got back to the manor the next day with my left arm in a sling, a mega-headache and new respect for things with wings.

Mr. and Mrs. McKenzie were really nice about the whole episode, especially considering that their two guests had managed to cause both a major search and a visit to the hospital. I figured it was probably the last time I'd be asked to go on holidays with Pepper.

I was lying down, kind of dozing, when Pepper and Hal crept into the bedroom.

Pepper said, "Hi," and then Hal said, "Hi." I blinked at them because talking made my head hurt more. Hal leaned over me and stared into my eyes.

"What are you doing?" Pepper asked him.

"I'm checking to see if she has pupils."

"Of course she has pupils. Everybody has pupils."

"I heard that when you have a concussion your pupils go way up inside your head."

"That's stupid."

I was glad Pepper was there so I wouldn't have to argue with Hal myself.

"Should I tell her?" Hal asked. "She's got pupils so she can't be too bad."

"Yeah, I think we should tell her."

Hal leaned close again. "Chris, can you hear me? Just blink if you can hear me. One blink for yes and two blinks for no."

"If she can't hear you, don't you think she wouldn't blink at all?" Pepper pointed out, which I thought was a pretty bright observation.

"Oh yeah," Hal said.

I blinked.

"Great," Hal grinned at me. "Well, as you know we went into the room—"

That was too much. I knew Hal had gone in and left me lying on the ground, but Pepper?

"You mean you just left me there, too?" I turned my head to look at Pepper, which was a big mistake because I almost passed out.

"Well... yeah," she looked at the floor, "but only for a few minutes."

I wanted to tell her what I thought about that, but my head was hurting too much and anyway Hal interrupted.

"So we got inside and started checking it out and at first it looked pretty ordinary: a big bed against one wall, a dresser and a desk and some pictures on the wall, the usual stuff. So we snooped around some more and finally we looked in the desk and guess what we found."

I didn't guess.

"There were scrapbooks and newspaper clippings and notes and file folders and everything in there. And every single clipping and piece of paper had something to do with one family. You wanna guess the name?"

I didn't want to so I shut my eyes.

"Jaglers!" Hal made his voice sound dramatic.

I opened my eyes. "Jaglers. I've heard that name."

"You sure have," Pepper nodded. "Do you remember where?"

"No," I said. Trying to remember things also made my head hurt.

"Leonard Livermore!" Hal announced.

"Remember? Leonard told us that Jaglers framed him and got him sent to jail for all those years," Pepper added.

"Oh yeah." Actually, it *was* kind of interesting news and I would have liked to sound a little more excited about it, but my head hurt and mostly I wanted to sleep. "Why would Mr. Cubbington-Smith have all that stuff about somebody who lived a couple of hundred years ago?"

"The clippings and the scrapbooks and stuff aren't about that guy," Pepper explained. "They're all about the modern-day Jaglers family."

"Yeah, there's lords and dukes and ladyships and one's a Member of Parliament, and there's a professor and—"

"But a lot of the stuff is about one person," Pepper leaned toward the bed and whispered. "Sir Alexander Jaglers. And guess what?"

"What's with all the guessing?" I asked.

"Sir Alexander Jaglers doesn't live too far from here," Hal pointed. "Straight down the road that goes right by this manor. Isn't this all just excellent? A real mystery. Cool, eh?"

"Listen, this is all fascinating, but if you two don't mind, I'd really like to sleep now." I wasn't trying to be rude. It's just that I was feeling crummier by the minute.

"Oh sure, okay," Pepper stood up. "Come on, Hal."

"Right." Hal leaned toward me again. "Nothing to worry about. Pepper and I will keep spying on Cubbington-Smith. You just go ahead and get better. You're doing great."

As they were leaving, I heard Pepper ask Hal how he knew I was "doing great."

"Simple," Hal answered. "She's got pupils, doesn't she?"

14

Simon Again

That night, Pepper and Hal were sitting on the edge of my bed, one on each side, trying to cheer me up. At least that's what I think they were doing. It wasn't working.

Hal was telling stupid jokes and Pepper was giving me all the information she'd picked up from books about vampires. I wasn't interested in what either of them had to say. To be honest, I was still thinking about how they'd left me lying on the ground under the yew tree.

"They don't go through doors and windows at all," Pepper was saying, "not like ghosts do. Vampires open them up and walk through them just like everybody else. But what happens is they sort of semi-hypnotize whoever is in the room before they come in, so it *seems* like they just floated through, see?"

I thought about asking Pepper how they hypnotized

people they couldn't see and who weren't even in the same room, but I decided not to. I noticed they didn't have the big garlic globs around their necks any more. That was something I did want to ask about.

I pointed. "Where's your garlic, you guys?"

"One of Pepper's books said it didn't make any difference," Hal said, "and I got tired of smelling like a sausage, so we got rid of it."

"But Simon said—" That's as far as I got. Suddenly the room became a lot cooler. All three of us knew we were about to receive a vampire visitor.

I decided to test Pepper's theory and concentrated as hard as I could on the door. But the next thing I knew, Simon was standing at the end of my bed. I still can't figure out how he got there. Maybe Pepper was right about the hypnotism thing.

Simon looked at the cast on my arm and the sling for a long time before he said anything.

"You are injured," he said at last.

"There's no fooling you, is there?" I answered without even trying to keep the bitterness out of my voice. After all, he was as much to blame for my broken collarbone as Pepper and Hal. We wouldn't have been climbing that stupid yew tree if we didn't have to report to Simon Chelling every couple of days. At least that's what I told myself.

"I'm sorry," he said. But I didn't believe him.

"That's okay," Hal told him.

I stared several daggers in my brother's direction.

"What have you learned?" Simon asked.

I wasn't ready to tell him anything just yet. "What was the idea of giving us the wrong directions to find Hal?" I demanded.

Simon looked at me. The look on his face wasn't a smile, but it wasn't unpleasant either, at least not too unpleasant.

"I wanted to see how you would conduct yourselves when faced with a challenge," he said.

"Thanks." I sat up and glared at him.

He didn't seem to care. He looked at Pepper and Hal. "Well?"

Pepper cleared her throat. "Uh... we followed Mr. Cubbington-Smith a couple of nights ago."

"From where?"

"We don't really know," Pepper answered. "It was after we found Hal—"

"Thanks to Leonard Livermore," I interrupted, "and no thanks to you."

Simon ignored me. He looked at Pepper and raised his eyebrows.

"We... we saw him on the street. And we followed him back here. He seemed very nervous."

"Like he thought he was being followed," Hal piped up. "By the way, we didn't see you. I thought you said you were watching him all night."

"Much of the time, yes." Simon looked thoughtful. "Then what?"

I threw a fake coughing fit, hoping to make the two of them shut up. I didn't want them to tell Simon about the mysterious room. It didn't work.

"We saw him later," Pepper jerked her thumb toward the wall, "coming out of the room between our two bedrooms." She lowered her voice. "They keep it locked. No one is allowed in there."

I coughed some more and made some pretty obvious signs—close the mouths, zip the lips, button the flaps, shut the yaps, et cetera. This time they noticed. Unfortunately, so did Simon.

He stared at me in a distinctly unfriendly way. I felt myself shudder.

Finally, he looked away and spoke. "Is there more?"

I slumped back on the bed and waited for my brother and my best friend to spill the beans about going into the room and what they'd found. But they surprised me.

"Nope, that's about it." Hal looked down at the floor as he lied.

Simon looked at Pepper, but she just shrugged. Then he turned to me again.

"How did you hurt yourself?" he asked.

The worst thing about Simon was that you always felt he knew the answers to his questions before he asked them. The *real* answers. Which made lying kind of a problem.

"I... uh... fell," I pulled the covers up around my shoulders. The room seemed to be getting colder all the time.

"And is that all you have to report?" Simon asked no one in particular.

"Uh... yeah," Pepper nodded. "We would have had more, but Christine got hurt so we were sort of... busy."

"Yeah," Hal added, "but if you come back in a few days I'm sure we'll have a lot more for you. We're just getting the hang of it."

"Getting the hang of it?" Simon raised his eyebrows again, which, come to think of it, was about the only way his expression ever changed.

"He means we're beginning to understand what you want us to do," I explained.

"Yeah," Hal bobbed his head up and down.

"Very good," Simon lowered the brows and nodded. "I shall be extremely... active... for the next little while so your diligent attention will be required. Do you understand?"

"Yeah... sure," Hal said. Pepper and I just nodded.

Then Simon was gone. All three of us held our breath and waited. When we were convinced that the vampire had actually left, we started to breathe again. Pepper stood up and walked around to the other side of the bed.

"I wonder what he meant by that," she glanced at me.

"You mean 'active'?" I shivered. "I don't think I want to know."

Hal pumped his fist in the air. "Man, this is what I call a holiday," he said as Pepper groaned and I covered my head with a pillow.

The Hound of the Baskervilles?

"Pretty neat the way we didn't tell Simon about our Jaglers discovery, eh?" Hal bounced on my bed, reminding me that I had a broken collarbone.

"Yeah, neat," I said through clenched teeth.

"You see, I was thinking ahead," he told me.

"Oh?"

"Yeah, to our next move."

I hated the sound of that. "Our next move?"

"Well, it's obvious, isn't it?"

"Not to me," Pepper said from the other bed.

"Or me," I agreed.

"The Jaglers Manor." Hal's tone of voice told us he thought we were slow for not figuring it out. "We've got to go over there and get inside and—"

"Forget it!" I held up my good arm. "No way. In your

dreams, pal."

"Calm down, Sis, just calm down," Hal lowered his voice. I hate it when he calls me that. I would have covered my ears to keep his irritating voice out, but having one arm in a sling meant I had to listen.

"Come over here, Pepper," he waved his arm in Pepper's direction, but she ignored him. "Okay, now listen," Hal went on anyway. "We're right on the edge of something big. We know that Cubbington-Smith is up to something, and that it involves Jaglers. We also know that it was the Jaglers family who framed Leonard, who has sworn to get revenge. It all fits." He smiled smugly, first at Pepper, then at me.

"What are you talking about?" I yelled. Hal put his finger to his lips to shush me, but I didn't shush. "Nothing fits. You find a few stupid papers in a locked room and suddenly you want to go breaking into somebody's house to look for who knows what. We could get ourselves arrested or shot or... people don't like other people sneaking into their houses to spy on them. And don't forget that we're not dealing only with people here. Let's not forget that we're up to our necks in vampires..."

"Chris... yuck." Pepper made a face.

I realized then what I'd said. "Yeah... well... it's true. If we go messing around, I'd hate to think what could happen to us."

"What you're forgetting is that we have to deliver some information to Simon when he shows up again in a couple of days." Hal stood up and started pacing around the room. I think he was trying to do his adult routine.

I wasn't buying it. "That doesn't mean we have to check out the neighbours," I told him. "All we're supposed to do is watch Mr. Cubbington-Smith."

Hal whirled around dramatically. "Who just happens to have a secret room full of stuff about somebody named Jaglers who just happens to have a connection with the vampires."

"He's right... sort of," Pepper nodded slowly.

Terrific! My best friend was siding with my lunatic brother... again.

"Look at this," I pointed at my sling. "Look at it! That's what your last brainwave about snooping did. And if you—"

"Chill, Sis. If you think about it, this could be the best way to get the vampires off our backs. Once they have their info, they won't need to bother us any more. Right?"

"No, I—"

Pepper interrupted me. "I hate to say it, but he's making sense, Chris."

"I don't care what you two say, I'm not going into that house." I tried to cross my arms, but you need two good ones to do that. "Do you hear me? No. Never. No way. Uh-uh. Nope. Negative. And also no, no, no."

Exactly twenty-four hours later, Pepper, Hal and I were

crouched behind a concrete wall that ran around the outside of the Jaglers place.

I peeked over the top of the wall and was not impressed by what I saw. The Cubbington-Smith manor may have been kind of weird, what with all the garlic and the secret room and everything, but compared to the Jaglers place, it was Disneyland.

The house we were looking at over the wall made a bleak first impression. I got the distinct feeling that the people who lived there were not going to be a lot of fun. There were lots of windows, but not a single light shone from any of them. Every room in the place was dark. The outside of the house was covered with ivy. But instead of being green and cheery like most ivy-covered walls, this one was brown. The ivy, like the house itself, looked dead.

I knew right away I shouldn't have let Pepper and Hal talk me into coming. Actually they didn't, I guess. It's just that once they told me they were going to the Jaglers estate with or without me, well, I couldn't just let the two of them go off and get themselves captured or... whatever, could I? Anyway, as we crouched by the wall, a small part of me started to think that this "adventure" was going to be even worse than the yew tree fiasco.

Oh, and one other thing about the house. I said there wasn't any light. That isn't quite right. There was one—a giant spotlight mounted on the top of the house. The beam moved all over the yard, which meant that sneaking up to the house without being seen was impossible. Whoever was in the house would be able to watch every move we made.

I turned to look at Hal and Pepper. They were now standing on tiptoes in an effort to see over the wall.

"Well, anybody have any bright ideas?" I asked.

"Nope," Pepper shrugged.

"You bet," Hal grinned.

"I was afraid of that." I looked back at the house. It looked evil in the moonless dark of the night. It wasn't cold out, but I shivered just the same.

"I don't suppose your idea has anything to do with going home and forgetting this whole thing, does it?" I looked at Hal.

"Naw!" He looked back at me. "Way better than that."

He waited for a response, but neither Pepper nor I could come up with anything so he went on.

"We split up."

Pepper looked at me and I looked at her. We both hated the plan already.

"It's the only way," Hal burbled on. "That way the light will never pick up all three of us at once. And we meet right below the big steeple thing over there." He pointed.

"That's a turret," Pepper said with no expression in her voice. I think she was finally starting to lose her longing for adventure. At least for *this* adventure.

"Right," Hal nodded, "that's what I said. We meet at the turret in five minutes. Check your watches."

"I don't have a watch," Pepper told him.

"Neither do I," I said, "and, by the way, neither do you."

"No problem. We just count one thousand one, one thousand two until we get to one thousand three hundred. Just make sure you're at the steeple thing when you get to one thousand three hundred."

"Terrific plan," I muttered.

"Yeah," said Pepper.

"Okay, let's spread out and get going."

Hal spread out. Pepper and I just shuffled around until we were about an arm's length away from each other. Then we climbed over the wall and started for the house. We moved using a combination of skipping, tiptoeing, slow-motion running and crouching down in a sort of duck walk. The whole time we kept cranking our heads around, trying to follow the arc from the spotlight. A couple of times we were lit up like Christmas trees. But the light moved on and there weren't any shouts or anything so I figured so far, so good. So far...

There was no sign of Hal. The only thing I did see was what looked like a well in the middle of the yard. A tall hedge ran in a semicircle around the far side of it.

Pepper and I crept up to the well, then made a dash for the hedge.

"What number are you up to?" Pepper asked as we crouched by the hedge.

"What?"

"The number. Remember, we were supposed to be

counting up to one thousand three hundred?"

"Oh yeah," I gasped at her between gulps of air. "I... uh... I sort of forgot."

"Me too."

We looked at each other and stepped carefully around the corner of the hedge. That's when *so far, so good* came to a sudden and very unpleasant end.

We found ourselves staring into the large, very nasty eyes—not to mention jaws—of the biggest dog I have ever seen. As a matter of fact, I've seen quite a few horses that weren't as big as that dog.

The dog growled. Pepper screamed. I can't remember exactly what I did, but I think a lot of it involved shaking... and hating my brother.

"It's... the... the Hound of the... Basker... villes," Pepper stammered.

Like I said before, she'd been reading a lot of Sherlock Holmes. Personally, I had no idea what the Hound of the Baskervilles looked like, but as I focused on the drooling jaws with teeth the size of popsicles, I figured this time Pepper could be right.

Except that we weren't at the Baskervilles' house. We were at the Jaglers'. But that thought didn't make me feel any better as I watched the dog take first one step toward us, then another!

Bad Dog

I took a step back.

The dog took a step forward.

I took another step back and looked around hoping to see someone, anyone—even Hal—who might be able to help.

Pepper was stepping backward with me. In fact, we probably looked like a musical dance number.

The dog stopped and crouched. The growling became more intense. I was sure that Pepper and I were about to become kibbles for the psycho hound.

Just then, someone whistled—one of those shrill whistles that only some people can make. In a split second the dog went from a crazed killer about to strike to Lassie. He lay down, stopped growling and tilted his head to one side as he looked at us.

He actually looked sort of cute. That is if a dog the size of a pickup truck can look cute.

I looked at Pepper. Even in the dark she looked white. I must have looked the same.

"Uh... who do you think whistled?" I asked her in a whisper.

"I don't know, but I've got a horrible feeling we'll be finding out pretty soon," she whispered back.

She was right.

For a few seconds the place got really quiet. The dog even quit panting. And Pepper and I almost stopped breathing.

"Ladies," a voice said.

I peered into the dark, trying to see who had spoken. I couldn't see a thing. Where was the stupid spotlight when you needed it? That's when I realized that the spotlight had gone out. No wonder it seemed so dark all of a sudden.

"Who are you?" I tried to sound calm.

"Who are *you*?" the voice asked.

"We're from out of town... and... uh... we're just visiting... and we were sort of... lost," I explained.

"Then it's a very good thing I found you," the voice said.

"Uh... yes... it is... thank you," I smiled, although I was pretty sure nobody would actually see the smile in the dark. "Well, I guess we should be getting on our way. Sorry to disturb you."

"Aren't you forgetting something?"

I should have known it wouldn't be that easy. "Uh... no, I don't think so," I said softly.

"Were there not three of you?" the voice asked in a way that gave me the shivers.

Hal, I thought to myself. "Oh yes, my little brother was lost too. In fact, we became separated in the dark."

Pepper spoke finally, in her sweetest voice. "Do you happen to know where he might be?"

"Oh yes." The voice sounded like it was coming closer. "Fortunately, I found him as well."

"Oh," I said.

"Oh-oh," Pepper said.

"He's in the house. No doubt he'll be very glad to be reunited with you."

"Uh... yeah." I decided to try a new approach. "I'm Christine Bellamy and this is my friend Pepper McKenzie. My brother's name is Hal and—"

"I know who you are," the voice said.

"Oh," I said again.

Finally, the person who was speaking came close enough to be seen. At first I was just glad it *was* a person. But as I got a closer look at his face, the meanest face I have ever seen—next to the dog's before he heard the whistle, that is—I wasn't so sure.

"We sure do appreciate you finding all of us like this," I smiled real hard. "If you could bring my brother out, we'll be moving along."

"I think it would be best if you were to join him in the house," the man said.

He wasn't smiling. In fact, he had a face that looked like it had never smiled. He was dressed all in black and he had black hair and a thin black moustache that looked as if it had been painted on real straight. Like somebody had used a marking pen and a ruler.

"Come this way, please," he said.

"What if we don't want to?" I crossed my arms (as much as I could with the sling) to show him I meant business. "We don't even know who you are."

"I am Count Jaglers." He took a step toward me, which made me very nervous.

"*Count* Jaglers," Pepper repeated, then looked at me. "Wasn't Dracula...a...a..."

"Count?" A nasty sneer flickered on Jaglers' face. Then it went out like a burned-out Christmas bulb. "Yes, he was. Count Dracula, a quite famous vampire."

"Are you...?" I swallowed. It was hard to tell in the dark.

"Vampire?" Jaglers finished the question. "No, although we have many common...interests."

"Well, you can't make us go in that house." I wanted to cross my arms again, but they were still crossed from before.

"No," he nodded slowly in agreement, "I suppose I can't, but I can be rather persuasive."

He whistled a low, short whistle and instantly the dog changed personality again. Goodbye Lassie, hello psycho hound.

Suddenly, going up to the house seemed like a pretty reasonable thing to do.

Prisoners!

Jaglers led the way and the dog followed. A little too closely if you ask me.

Once in the house, Pepper and I were taken to a huge room, very much like the one we'd first been in at the Cubbington-Smith manor. Except this one wasn't cozy. No, not cozy at all.

There was a huge high-backed chair in the middle of the room facing away from us. When we came around to its front side, there was Hal looking most unhappy.

On the floor right in front of him was another dog, an exact replica of the psycho hound. This one never stopped looking at Hal, even when we approached the chair. Its mouth was open, giving us a good look at its massive, drooling jaws.

Hal was quieter than I can ever remember him being. Quieter and paler. Assuming we survived this latest crisis,

I had a feeling he might not be so eager in the future to embark on all these adventures.

Jaglers told Pepper and me to sit on the floor, one on either side of Hal. I thought of a couple of wisecracks about gentlemen giving up their seats for ladies, but I was pretty sure our host wouldn't appreciate comedy. I sat. So did Pepper.

"Now, my young visitors," Jaglers was rubbing his hands together in a way I didn't like, "what to do with you? Of course, that depends on whether you decide to give up that ridiculous tale of yours about being lost and tell me the truth."

For once, even without communicating, it turned out that my best friend, my brother and I were all on the same wavelength. None of us spoke.

"I said, I want to know why you are snooping around my grounds." Jaglers' voice was getting louder.

"Perhaps I should explain something," he said as he came toward us. "The law is on my side in such matters as these. Upstanding citizen discovers intruders—that's how it will read in the papers. Unhappily, the trained guard dogs ripped them apart before his lordship could stop them. Unfortunate but—"

"You can't keep us here," I yelled. "Pepper's parents know exactly where we are. We told them we were coming over here to...to...introduce ourselves...so when we don't show up, you're going to be in so much trouble..."

"Yeah, and not only that but we know all about your family and how one of your ancestors framed Mr. Livermore too."

That, of course, came from Hal.

If we'd had any chance at all of getting out of there, my brother had just killed it. And maybe us too.

I looked at Jaglers. His eyes seemed to become even darker than they'd been before. I was pretty sure that the three of us were spending our last hours on earth.

He stepped back and gave us that evil sneer he was so good at. "Perhaps I will make a phone call." He ran a hand over his hair and I waited for him to wipe the grease on his pants. "I'll call Miss McKenzie's parents. It shouldn't be difficult at all to find out if they know where you are. If, as I suspect, they have no idea where their little darlings have run off to . . . well," he rubbed his hands together again, "then, I'll know just how to deal with the situation, won't I? Oh, and just in case you should have any foolish thoughts about escaping, I'll leave you with Max and Killer." He chuckled. "Believe me, you'll be in good paws." He seemed to think that was real funny. When he stopped chortling, he whistled, a different one than before and both dogs went into alert mode—lots of snarling and drooling. Max leaned forward, showed us his fangs and even licked his lips. Killer looked like he was hoping one of us would try something.

"I'll be back momentarily," Jaglers said in a sickeningly cheerful voice as he left the room.

I was almost afraid to move, but I decided to try turning my head very slowly to the left so I could look at Hal and Pepper. They were sitting as still as I was except for the shaking, which all three of us were doing quite a lot of.

I looked back at Max and Killer. It was clear that if any of us made a dash for the door, the dogs would be delighted to put those humongous jaws into action.

"Nice Max," I whispered. "Good Killer."

The growls became a little louder.

"Anybody have an idea?" I said without taking my eyes off the dogs.

"Uh... not actually... not this time," Hal whispered back.

"Nope," Pepper added in a voice so soft I could barely hear her.

I was about to suggest we say our final goodbyes to each other when something totally strange—and totally excellent—happened. The room grew colder—just like it did whenever Simon Chelling showed up. I never thought I'd be overjoyed to see a vampire, but I found myself looking forward to Simon's appearance like a kid waiting for Santa.

That's why I wasn't quite ready for what happened next. It wasn't Simon who suddenly appeared in the room. It was Leonard Livermore!

I could have kissed him. Well, not quite, but I was pretty happy when the old vampire appeared, all hunched over like the trip had been hard on him. Even so, he was smiling, almost chuckling. But the best part was Max and

Killer. They went scurrying into the corner with their tails between their legs and crouched down on their bellies with their paws over their big faces.

"Good evening, young friends," Leonard looked at each of us.

Pepper and I jumped up. "Awright," Pepper yelled and I held up my one good arm in a salute. And Hal—you wouldn't have believed him. The guy who had heaped all the abuse on Leonard the last time we saw him rushed over and gave him a high-five. I'm pretty sure *that* had never happened to Leonard before.

"We had better be going," he told us when we'd finished celebrating. "Your host will be back soon."

We followed him out into a hall and around a corner. After that I was pretty much lost since Jaglers' manor was even bigger than Mr. Cubbington-Smith's. But finally we were outside. I was never so glad in my life to look up and see a huge orange full moon. The spotlight was still out, which made me even happier.

We hurried along behind Leonard until we were beyond the manor's outer wall. We no sooner got there than the spotlight started playing its nasty beam around the grounds again.

Pepper looked back at the house. "Jaglers must have discovered we're gone."

"I'll bet his brain is fried trying to figure out how we got past those dogs," Hal grinned.

"Thanks, Leonard." I turned to the old vampire. "You saved us for sure."

"Yes, there's no doubt he would have done you harm," Leonard frowned.

"What brought you here tonight?" Pepper asked.

"Yeah, how could you have known?"

"Simon sent me. He said you were in some difficulty and needed help," Leonard smiled. "He also said something about owing you one."

"He must've been following us," Pepper looked at me.

I shrugged. "Maybe. Or maybe he was watching Mr. Cubbington-Smith and saw us sneak off to Jaglers' house. Anyway he's right—he owed us one after that lovely evening we spent in the tunnels. But why couldn't he have rescued us himself?"

"He mentioned that he had other urgent business," Leonard told us, turning as he said it, "and so do I. You should be able to get home safely now."

"But..." I began, but it didn't do any good. He was gone, in that maddening way vampires had of just disappearing.

"Wow, what an amazing night!" Hal was practically jumping up and down.

"Yeah, right," I glared at him. "We were close to being history back there, in case you didn't notice. Now let's get home before Jaglers lets the dogs outside the wall."

That thought seemed to bring Hal a little closer to reality and we started for home at a walk-trot. We didn't talk much. I think all three of us were trying to get some kind of handle on what was going on.

Personally, I had to admit I didn't have a clue. Good vampires, bad vampires, a frame-up for a murder that happened a couple of centuries before, a secret room in one manor and a nasty neighbour with killer dogs in another. I thought as hard as I could but didn't come up with any ideas.

We were almost home when Hal made what I had to admit was a pretty good suggestion.

"I think it's time we had a talk with Mr. Cubbington-Smith." He twirled his ball cap around a couple of times. "I mean, we don't have to tell him we've been spying on him, just that we've found out a few things by accident and want to know what's going on."

"What happens if he tells us to take a hike?" Pepper asked.

"So what? We won't have lost anything."

They both looked at me. "It might not be a bad idea," I nodded. "At this point, I just wish I had some clue about what's happening around here. This is all just too weird and I'm getting really tired of it."

We decided that we would confront Mr. Cubbington-Smith the first chance we got, figuring the next morning after breakfast would be as good a time as any.

It turned out we didn't have to wait that long. We had just tiptoed in the front door and closed it behind us. We glanced up the stairs to make sure that the coast was clear. There, like a slow-motion replay of that other time, was Mr. Cubbington-Smith sneaking out of the locked bedroom.

A Three-Hundred-Year-Old Story

I figured we'd maybe follow him up to his room, knock politely on the door and, when he answered, say something like, "Excuse me, Mr. Cubbington-Smith, we were wondering, if it isn't too much trouble, if you could tell us what the heck is going on."

That, of course, isn't how it went at all.

"Yo!" It was Hal who yelled. "Yo, Mr. C.! What do you think you're doing?"

I thought Mr. Cubbington-Smith was going to have a heart attack. He spun around and grabbed the railing as if to keep from falling down. Finally, he spotted us at the bottom of the stairs. At first he didn't say anything. He just took a couple of deep breaths.

After a moment or two had passed, the corners of his

mouth turned up a very little bit as he tried to smile. "Upon my word," he said, "you gave me a start."

I was busy giving my brother a dirty look, but as usual he wasn't paying any attention. He started up the stairs two at a time with Pepper right behind him. I decided I better get up there too, before I missed out on something.

But when we got to the top of the staircase none of us could think of anything to say, not even Hal. So the three of us just looked at Mr. Cubbington-Smith, who looked back at us.

It was Pepper who finally managed to break the silence.

"Uh..." she said, which wasn't that much help.

"You wanted something?" Mr. Cubbington-Smith seemed to have regained his cool.

"Um... actually, yes," I said. "We were hoping you might be able to..." I looked around. "Maybe we should talk in our bedroom," I whispered.

"Fine. If you wish."

Mr. Cubbington-Smith followed us into the room Pepper and I had been sharing. Once inside, we had another attack of uh's and um's. It looked like it was up to me.

"Mr. Cubbington-Smith, we appreciate your hospitality and everything, but there's some really strange stuff happening and we'd like to know what's going on."

"What sort of strange... stuff?" he asked, just to stall for time I figured.

"Well, for starters," Hal joined in, "there's the room we just saw you come out of... the one that's locked up all the time."

"Yeah," Pepper nodded, "and there are vampires coming and going around here like the place was a video store or something."

"Uh... which vampires?" he asked in a voice not much louder than a whisper.

"Well, Simon Chelling," I said. "And the rest of those vampires. I guess they're the good ones, at least that's what he told us and—"

"You... know about the other vampires?"

"The renegades?" Hal shrugged. "The ones that kill people just for the fun of it? Yeah, we know about them."

Mr. Cubbington-Smith slowly lowered himself down onto one of the beds. He stared at the floor for a long time, not saying anything. Finally, he looked up and stared at each of us for a few seconds.

"You're right," he said finally. "You have a right to know what's going on. I'll try to explain it to you."

Pepper and I sat on the bed opposite Mr. Cubbington-Smith and Hal sat cross-legged on the floor.

"Before I say a word, it's very important that you agree not to speak of these things to anyone. Not to the police or anyone, do you understand?"

"Why not the police?" I asked.

"If you've seen the vampires, then you must know that

the police are absolutely powerless to control them in any way. If you go to the police, it's possible—in fact, quite likely—that all of us could end up dead."

"We won't say anything, honest." I looked at Pepper and Hal and they both nodded to show they agreed.

Mr. Cubbington-Smith took a deep breath and let it out slowly. "The story begins almost three hundred years ago. An ancestral aunt of mine lived here in this manor. She and her brother were the only children of my great-great-great-great-grandparents. Her name was Lady Pamela Cubbington-Smith and she fell in love with a young Scotsman who farmed a small piece of land not far from here.

"At first, her father disapproved of the marriage since the Scotsman, whose name was MacPherson, was not of noble blood. But eventually the young man's honesty, kindness and hard work won him over. That and the fact that MacPherson and Lady Pamela obviously loved each other very much."

Pepper and I were really getting into the story, but Hal had begun to fidget. Love stories just weren't his thing. Luckily, Mr. Cubbington-Smith didn't seem to notice.

"There was, unfortunately, a complication," he continued. "Someone else in the district was also in love with Lady Pamela, someone who *was* of noble blood but not of noble character—"

"Jaglers!" Hal blurted.

Mr. Cubbington-Smith's eyebrows went up in surprise. "You know about him?"

"Some," I nodded, "but there's a lot we don't know. Go ahead, tell us the rest."

"A few days before Lady Pamela and MacPherson were to be married, the Scotsman was found face down in a shallow lagoon on his farm. There was a knife in his back. Though many people suspected Jaglers of simply eliminating the competition, the evidence all pointed to a young soldier who was home on furlough, a man named..."

Mr. Cubbington-Smith stopped because Hal had opened his mouth to speak.

"Do you know this part too?" our host asked.

"Uh-huh," Hal answered. "Leonard Livermore, right?"

"Is there any of this you *don't* know?" Mr. Cubbington-Smith sounded a bit peeved.

"Lots," I assured him. "We didn't know anything about Lady Pamela."

"That's right," Pepper added. "Please keep going."

"All right," Mr. Cubbington-Smith stood up and began to walk around the room. "The man, Livermore, spent the rest of his days in ... wait a minute, how do you know about him?"

"We ... uh ... we ... met him," I said.

"You met Livermore?" Mr. Cubbington-Smith slumped back down on the bed. "But he's ..."

"Yeah, we know. Vampire."

"Oh dear, oh dear." Mr. Cubbington-Smith became quite flustered again, the way he had been when we saw him coming out of the closed room.

"It's okay," Pepper said. "He's actually a pretty nice guy. He told us all about being wrongly accused and how he still wants to get revenge on Jaglers, even though Jaglers has been dead for a couple of centuries."

I flexed my injured arm, which was starting to stiffen up. "After meeting the current Count Jaglers, I'll bet there's a pretty big similarity between him and the one that killed MacPherson and framed Leonard."

Mr. Cubbington-Smith looked dazed. "How did you learn all this?"

"Just picked up a few things during our evening walks," Pepper smiled. I was glad she didn't go into detail about our encounters with Leonard and Jaglers.

"Is there more to the story?" I asked.

"Yes," he nodded his head sadly. "After MacPherson was murdered, Lady Pamela was overcome with grief. She went into her room and never came out again. She just... died."

Pepper sniffed and I felt a tear in the corner of my eye. Hal's reaction was a little different.

"Jaglers... what a jerk!" He slammed his fist on his knee. I had to agree with my brother.

All of us were wrapped up in our own thoughts for a while. It was Pepper who spoke next.

"Is the room next door...was that Lady Pamela's room?" she asked.

Mr. Cubbington-Smith nodded. "Yes. It's been closed up ever since her death."

"Can I ask a question now?" Hal stood up.

"Certainly."

"How come you have all that stuff about Count Jaglers in there...all those clippings and stuff?"

If Mr. Cubbington-Smith was surprised that we knew about the things in the closed room, he didn't show it.

"The Jaglers family and my own have not been on good terms since the whole episode with Lady Pamela. I've spent my lifetime, as did my father and his father before him, trying to find evidence that would prove who MacPherson's real murderer was. Especially as that person was also responsible for the death of Lady Pamela."

"Isn't that kind of impossible?" I asked. "I mean, after all this time, hasn't the evidence disappeared?"

"One would think so, of course," Mr. Cubbington-Smith replied, "although there are records, correspondence and the like that still exist. I was almost ready to give up a few months ago when I learned that a letter written to Lady Pamela's father by another soldier, a friend of Leonard Livermore, still existed. I had heard of the letter before, of course, but thought—as did everyone else—that it had long since disappeared. The letter supposedly says that this soldier was with Leonard when MacPherson was killed and could, therefore, prove Leonard's innocence. It went on to say that the soldier was paid a large sum of money to lie.

"As a result, Leonard Livermore was convicted and sent to jail for the rest of his life. Many years later the soldier regretted what he had done and wrote to Lady Pamela's father to set the record straight. You can probably guess who paid the soldier to lie in the first place."

"Jaglers!" we yelled in unison.

"Exactly."

Something still didn't make sense to me. "Once Lady Pamela's father received that letter, wouldn't Leonard have been set free?"

"The letter vanished before it could be acted upon. It was the possibility, however slight, that it might one day turn up that kept my ancestors working at solving the mystery. And me, for the matter." Mr. Cubbington-Smith sighed then and looked off into space. "And now to be so close . . . to righting a centuries-old wrong *and* restoring the family's honour—"

"Then Jaglers must want that letter as much as you do," I said.

"Of course," Mr. Cubbington-Smith nodded. "If it should fall into his hands, then the truth will never come out."

"How did you find out that the letter's still around?" Pepper asked.

Mr. Cubbington-Smith cleared his throat a couple of times and looked very uncomfortable. "That's one part of the story I think it would be best to keep to myself."

I had an idea. "I think I know where you got the information."

He looked at me but didn't say anything.

"The vampires?" I said.

He hesitated, then nodded. "Yes," he said softly, "the vampires... the... 'renegades,' as you called them."

I could hear both Hal and Pepper exhale.

"They told me they have the letter. I don't know how it came to be in their possession, and I don't suppose it really matters. They came to me and told me if I wanted it back I'd have to do whatever they asked."

"Which was?" I asked.

"To gather information on the other group of vampires... to spy on them. When I told them I wouldn't, they threatened to give the letter to Jaglers and... and to kill me."

"Wait a minute." Pepper looked at me. "Simon's one of the *good* vampires and he's blackmailing us to spy on Mr. Cubbington-Smith. And the *bad* vampires are blackmailing him to spy on the good vampires. Who's following who around here?"

"What did you say?" Mr. Cubbington-Smith stood up.

"I said..." That's when Pepper realized what she'd said. "Uh... oops." She put her hand over her mouth.

"We're sorry, sir," I said, "but Simon thinks you're working with the bad vampires and..." I stopped as Mr. Cubbington-Smith walked slowly to the window.

He looked out for a long time, then turned to us. I'm not sure, but it looked like he had tears in his eyes. When he spoke his voice was so soft I could hardly hear it.

"I've been able to find most of the daytime resting places for the... good vampires. I was planning to give that information to the... others later tonight."

I looked at him. "But if you do that Simon and the others could be exposed to daylight and killed. The renegade vampires might even force you to do it."

"I... I hadn't thought of that." Mr. Cubbington-Smith shook his head. "I know it was wrong to get involved with all of this, but I didn't know what else to do. How can you stop these...?"

It was a very difficult question to answer. One thing was for sure: none of us had the solution. I stood up.

"We need to talk to Simon," I said. "Right away. He's the only one who can sort all this out." I looked at Mr. Cubbington-Smith. "We have to tell him that you're not really working with the bad vampires, that they're blackmailing you."

"But how do we find Simon?" Pepper asked.

"I don't know," I said.

"I do," Hal piped up. "There's one guy that can help us find him."

"Oh no," I groaned. I knew what my brother was going to suggest. And even worse, I knew he was right.

"Who?" Pepper hadn't figured it out yet.

"Leonard Livermore, of course," Hal said.

"But... that means we have to go back down in those tunnels," Pepper's voice sounded like I felt.

"I know," I said. "I don't want to go down there either, but Hal's right. I don't know if we have much choice."

"What are you talking about?" Mr. Cubbington-Smith looked totally lost.

"Leonard Livermore and the other good vampires sleep in tunnels under Hyde Park."

"Yes, I was aware of that," Mr. Cubbington-Smith nodded. "That was part of the information I was going to pass on tonight."

"That's where we have to go to find Leonard," Hal told him.

"You... you've been there... in the tunnels?"

"Uh... yeah, I guess you could say so," Hal said. "It was no picnic."

"I can quite imagine," said Mr. Cubbington-Smith.

"I don't know if I can go down there again," Pepper whined.

"We have to," I told her. "I don't want to go either, but if we don't find Leonard in a hurry... things could get pretty bad around here."

Pepper swallowed and nodded slowly. "I guess so," she said.

"Perhaps I should go along," Mr. Cubbington-Smith offered.

"Thanks," I said, "but I think we'd better do this alone. Leonard's used to us and we have a pretty good idea where to go."

"This time, let's take a flashlight," Pepper suggested.

"With extra batteries," I added.

My brother, who never misses a chance to be dramatic, spread his arms. "Okay, boys and girls, it's showtime," he announced.

That kid really gets on my nerves sometimes.

Back in Black

All three of us stood staring at Peter Pan's statue for quite a while. It was like we were hoping it would come to life and do something spectacular. Almost anything would do as long as it kept us from going down into the tunnels again.

But, of course, nothing happened. The stone guy didn't move, didn't flinch, didn't even blink. And after a few minutes (quite a few, actually) of staring and wishing, Pepper, Hal and I looked at each other, shrugged and started tracing the line from Peter's heel to the secret entrance in the bushes.

The flashlight helped, of course. We found the stumps and the handle quite easily and in a few seconds we were descending the steps. We were moving very slowly, even with the light.

Unfortunately, it wasn't long before we had to go even more slowly. That's because Hal, who insisted on carrying the flashlight, tripped on a crack in the cement before we'd even gone one-quarter of the way down the first tunnel. The flashlight hit the floor with a crash that sounded like a gunshot. There was one bright flash and then nothing. Actually, worse than nothing—darkness, total, black and everywhere.

I could tell that Hal felt bad about destroying our only source of light, so I didn't say anything—not even one snide remark. Pepper wasn't quite as willing to let him off the hook.

"Way to go, worm-brain," was the way she put it.

"Listen to the rocket scientist." Hal didn't miss the chance to return the sarcasm.

I didn't feel like listening to them arguing in the dark. "Cool it, you two," I told them. "What we need here is a plan. Anybody have any ideas?"

"Uh-uh," Pepper said.

"Nope," said Hal.

"Do you remember how much farther we went up the tunnel after we met Leonard?" I asked Pepper.

"I can't even remember which way we went."

I should have known that the crash from the breaking flashlight had been loud enough to get someone's attention. It did. The next voice I heard didn't belong to Pepper or to my brother. And, unfortunately, it didn't belong to Leonard Livermore either.

"Ah, we meet again," it said as a match flared and a lantern was lit. The face of Count Jaglers emerged in the soft glow of the lantern light. And next to him—one on each side—were two very scary-looking guys. Even without an introduction, I was positive we had just met our first bad vampires.

"Oops," Hal said.

Pepper and I didn't say anything. To be honest, I couldn't think of one thing to say that fit the situation. The only good thing was that Jaglers hadn't brought the dogs. I guess he figured that with those two goons along, Max and Killer would be unnecessary.

I still hadn't gotten a close look at the two vampires' faces, but I didn't really have to. They were big and they were mean—that much I was sure of. They kind of reminded me of a couple of motorcycle gang types without all the leather.

Of course, I was also trying *not* to spend a lot of time looking at the two of them. I absolutely did not want to be hypnotized—or whatever it is that vampires do to their victims—by these two.

I looked over at Pepper, and what I saw wasn't good—not good at all. She must have snuck a look at one of the goons because she was standing there like a zombie and kind of offering her neck to the creep. One of the vampires started toward her.

I screamed. It was partly out of fear and partly because if Leonard was anywhere in the tunnels, I wanted to get his attention.

Jaglers laughed. "Foolish little urchin," he said. "Do you think we'd be here if we hadn't taken care of that old idiot first?"

"You suck!" Hal yelled, which only made Jaglers laugh even more.

"Now, what I plan to do is keep two of you as hostages. That way I'll have something to offer. As for the other one, I think my friends here are in need of nourishment. And I see that your companion appears to be most willing to oblige."

The biggest and ugliest of the two vampires was in front of Pepper now. He took hold of her shoulders and leaned toward her, drawing his lips back as he did. I remember Mr. Cubbington-Smith saying that only movie vampires had fangs. If that's true, then this vampire could have had a pretty good career in film.

Every once in a while my little brother does something that surprises me. A lot of the time the surprises are the unpleasant kind. This time, though, I was really proud of him. Hal kicked Jaglers in the shin! Kicked him hard, as a matter of fact. I think Hal was probably trying to get everybody's mind off of Pepper's blood. It was a nice try.

Unfortunately, it didn't work. At least not for long.

Jaglers howled in pain, grabbed his leg and hopped up and down for a few seconds. But when he stopped doing those things he was mad. Real mad. Jaglers' mouth was doing a lot of the same things Max's mouth had done earlier that night at the mansion.

"Well?" he screamed at the vampire who was just inches from Pepper's neck. "What are you waiting for?"

"Hold it!" I screamed. "We know where the letter is. If you don't let her go this second I swear you'll never find it."

I knew it was a gamble. But Jaglers had talked about hostages—something to offer. Offer for what? I could think of only one thing that could be that important to him.

Jaglers looked very surprised. "Wait." He forced himself between the vampire and Pepper, something I can't say I'd have wanted to do. "You can do this later," he spoke softly to the vampire. "In fact, I promise you more than just her."

As he said that he turned and looked at me in a way that sent a shiver through my body. "What do you know about the letter?"

"Everything," I said. "We know everything—that the letter proves Leonard was innocent, that he didn't kill Mr. MacPherson and that it was your ancestor, Count Jaglers, who really did it."

What I didn't know was this: if the renegades were blackmailing Jaglers, promising he'd get the letter if he did what they wanted, wouldn't they have told him they had the letter? Maybe not. Maybe they had been secretive about the letter's location. Or maybe they had told him that Mr. Cubbington-Smith had it, but that they could get it. Unlikely, but it was my only shot. If I could just make Jaglers believe that we had somehow gained possession of the letter... I tried to make my face look confident, which was about the last thing I actually felt.

Jaglers seemed to be thinking about what I'd said. "Who else knows about this?" he asked.

I realized this was a tricky question. If I said we were the only ones, he might decide that having us dead (and silent) was better than using us as hostages. And if I said we'd told lots of people about the letter, then we wouldn't be all that valuable to him, which could mean we'd never get out of this tunnel. And other people could be put in danger too.

So I said, "It's none of your business, creep."

"Awright, Sis!" Hal yelled. He doesn't usually hear me speak that way to people—except him, of course.

"If you somehow found the letter, why wouldn't you have simply given it to that idiot Cubbington-Smith?" Jaglers glared at each of us in turn. "He is your host, after all."

I didn't have an answer for that one. I looked down at the floor and tried to make my mind think... think...

"Simple," Pepper's voice was filled with the confidence I'd been wishing for. She must have snapped out of the trance when Jaglers called off vampire-boy. "You don't think your vampire friends are the only ones capable of blackmail, do you?"

The corners of Jaglers' mouth curled up in an evil sneer. "And what exactly is it you want in return for the letter?"

"A million dollars!" Hal blurted out the words before Pepper and I could reply.

"We are prepared to let you have the letter if you'll promise us our freedom and safety... from them," I inclined my head in the direction of the two vampires.

"Of course, of course," Jaglers said, much too quickly and with way too much nodding. "You have my word as a gentleman."

Pepper and I looked at each other. "Yeah, right," she said under her breath.

"Well, where is it? And you'd better be quick about telling me." Jaglers took a step toward me.

"It's... it's at Mr. Cubbington-Smith's house. We... we... hid it." I didn't really know what to say, but I knew I had to say something. I was really just stalling for time, in the hope that something might happen to get us out of the mess we were in.

I guess Jaglers must have figured that's what I had in mind. "One of you will stay here... with Lucas," he said, turning his head to indicate the vampire who had taken such an interest in Pepper's neck. Lucas opened his mouth, which I imagine was his way of showing he liked the suggestion.

"Oh no," I said. "If all of us don't go, then you can forget the letter. There's no way Pepper is staying behind... with that." I pointed at the vampire.

"All right." Jaglers' voice reminded me of Max's growls. "But this better not take long. We go to the house. We get the letter. No stalling. No more talking. Am I understood?"

"Yes," I said. "You're understood."

Jaglers turned to lead the way out of the tunnel. I was glad we weren't taking the route that went by all the coffins. The two vampires were following right behind, so Pepper, Hal and I stayed close to Jaglers. Even though he was ten times a creep, he was better than Lucas and his friend.

We walked/ran back to the manor. Jaglers apparently thought the six of us might look a little suspicious in a taxi. That was fine with me since I wasn't crazy about the idea of being in close quarters with the three of them anyway.

The trip was silent except for Jaglers hustling us along every few minutes. I tried to use the time to figure some things out—like a way to help us escape.

Jaglers was easy to figure out. He wanted to protect his family name and would stop at nothing to do so. The vampires' part was pretty basic too. The "good" and "bad" vampires were locked in a feud, one that could end up with the destruction of an entire group. But it was the vampires' involvement with *people* that really had me puzzled. What was it Simon had said? Some humans were supplying vampires with daytime hiding places and maybe even some victims in return for help in knocking off their enemies.

Yeah, I could see Jaglers helping out the vampires and even—I shuddered at the thought—bringing unsuspecting victims to them. And it was easy to imagine Jaglers suggesting that the vampires would be doing him a favour if they just happened to eliminate Peter Cubbington-Smith!

Of course! That had to be it. Mr. Cubbington-Smith was definitely Jaglers' enemy. Even worse, Mr. Cubbington-Smith was the one guy who could reveal the truth about the murder of Lady Pamela's fiancé. But if Mr. Cubbington-Smith was the enemy, why hadn't the maverick vampires done away with him long ago? Even with the good vampires following him at night, there must have been opportunities for someone like Lucas to . . . you know.

I kept coming back to the letter. Mr. Cubbington-Smith didn't have it, but Jaglers didn't know that. And I was beginning to suspect that the renegades didn't know where it was. Otherwise, my little charade wouldn't have gotten this far. But in order to keep their own plan in action—the plan to blackmail Jaglers—they had to keep their mouths shut. Lucas and his sidekick had no choice: they had to let Jaglers think that the letter was at Mr. Cubbington-Smith's manor so they could keep using him until . . . until they got rid of Simon and the rest of the good ones.

Finally, it was starting to make sense. The bad vampires couldn't have cared less about some letter written before lots of them even *were* vampires. But if it would help them get power over their own enemies, that was another matter. So they tell Jaglers *and* Mr. Cubbington-Smith that they know where the letter is. That way, they have both men under their control—working for them in their feud with the other side.

We were getting close to the manor. Even though I was fairly sure I had some idea of what was going on, I was no closer to a brainwave that would save us.

The house was in total darkness. Naturally, it would be, I thought to myself. I had no idea what time it was, but it felt like we'd been up all night. I would have given anything to climb into my bed back in Riverbend and sleep for a long time. The thought occurred to me that if I didn't come up with an idea real soon, I might end up sleeping for a *very* long time.

Jaglers wanted to go in the back door. We crept around the side of the house, passed under the yew tree—the *famous* yew tree—and arrived at the back entrance. The door was open. I had been hoping it would be locked and that it would take us forever to get in. Nope. Jaglers pushed Pepper, then Hal and then me through the door.

When we were all inside—in a room that was once used as a combined porch and servants' quarters—Jaglers grabbed my good arm.

"All right, where is it?"

"It's . . . uh . . . in the . . . uh . . . library," I managed to stammer.

I had no particular reason to pick that room. I needed to tell him something, though, and I guess maybe I figured if I was going to have all the blood sucked out of me, a library was as good a place as any for it to happen.

We crept down and around the twisting hall and finally got to the library's big double doors. Jaglers pushed one open and led the way inside.

"Get the letter," he snarled at me.

I wandered over to the shelves. Pepper and Hal stayed close to me. "I... uh... think I put it in a volume of Longfellow." I moved along the shelves until I came to the L's.

"Let's see, Lewis, Lithgow, Lytton... uh." I was stalling again, but I was also getting panicky. I knew that our time had just about run out—no matter how much more goofing around I did.

"Hurry it up!" Jaglers came up alongside me and glared at the books. "There. Longfellow's right there."

He grabbed *Hiawatha* from the shelves and raced through the pages, occasionally shaking the book by its binding. I was watching and hoping that by some magic, a piece of paper might fall out.

But, of course, nothing did.

"Oh, geez," I smacked my forehead with the palm of my hand. "Did I say Longfellow? That was the *first* place I hid it. But I moved it, just to be, you know... careful. I put it in a book by Sir Walter Scott."

Jaglers moved toward the S section.

"Then, of course, I moved it again," I said. "Yes, I decided the best place for that letter would be in a book of poetry by Elizabeth Barrett Browning. You know, love and all that stuff."

Jaglers turned to face me. I think he wanted to kill me right then and there.

"Honest," I said, "it's in the Browning poems. I... I didn't move it again after that."

The good thing about the Browning section was that it was too high to reach. Jaglers pointed to the ladder at the far end of the shelves. "Get it," he ordered.

Lucas went for the ladder, set it against the bookshelves and climbed up. This was our last chance. As he was reaching for the book of Browning poems, I pushed the ladder as hard as I could. For a second it teetered, then went crashing to the floor, taking Lucas with it.

"Come on!" I yelled, and Pepper, Hal and I made for the door.

That's when I got two big surprises. First of all, I found out how fast a vampire can move. Believe me, it's very fast. Lucas' partner got to the door and closed it before we had taken more than a couple of steps.

Hal said the first words I'd heard from him in a very long time. "I think we're in trouble now," he said very softly.

The other surprise was an even bigger one. Until that very minute, we hadn't seen the face of the second vampire. It had stood in the shadows down in the tunnels, and I'd been avoiding looking at both of them ever since. Now I got a good, long look, and when I did, I almost collapsed. The second vampire was a woman!

She was big and anything but beautiful, but I still

figured we might have a better chance with her than with Lucas or Jaglers. Maybe she'd had a bit of kindness in her when she was alive and maybe that spark of kindness still flickered in her heart.

"Please," I begged, "please let us go. We'll never tell on you if you'll just..."

I was wrong about the kindness part. She didn't say anything, but she did open her mouth and draw her lips back, just like Lucas had in the tunnel. We backed up. Over my shoulder I could see Lucas getting up off the floor. He wasn't hurt, but he looked awfully mad.

Jaglers walked slowly across the room toward us. "Well," he rubbed his hands together, "I guess your little game is over, isn't it? I think the time has come for Annie and Lucas to do what vampires do best."

With that same unbelievable speed, Annie grabbed Hal and lifted him off the floor. Lucas rushed to Pepper to finish what he'd started earlier. Both Pepper and Hal must have been in some kind of trance because neither of them fought or yelled or anything. Jaglers grabbed my sore shoulder and slapped his hand over my mouth to keep me from screaming before it was my turn. I remember having this strange thought: I wondered which one of the vampires would drain my blood. Weird, the thoughts a person has at a time like that.

I wasn't sure I'd ever find out. Jaglers' grip on me was causing my shoulder to throb. Between the pain and the fear, I could feel myself starting to pass out. And that's when one more surprise took place. Both doors to the library were flung open and there stood Simon Chelling!

20 Jaglers—and Jugulars

And behind Simon was Mr. Cubbington-Smith. In all the frightening chaos of the night, I had completely forgotten about Mr. Cubbington-Smith, who had stayed behind when we went to the tunnels. He must have found Simon. Or maybe Simon found him. I didn't care how it had happened. They were both here and that meant that we just might have a chance.

"Let go of the children," Simon ordered the two vampires who were about to bite into the necks of my brother and my best friend.

"Not bloody likely," Lucas turned to Simon. It was the first words I'd heard either of the two vampires say, and an interesting choice of words it was.

At least Lucas seemed momentarily distracted. But Pepper was still standing like a limp rag doll with her head thrown back to expose her neck.

"Who's gonna stop me?" Lucas grinned a horrible grin. "You? You're nothin' but a bleedin' pup."

Again with the blood references. Talk about a one-track mind. Actually, Lucas had a point. He towered over Simon. He was huge and he looked strong. Annie wasn't exactly a shrimp herself.

"I'll tell you what, pup," Lucas' grin grew bigger and more disgusting. "I'll let you watch me." He turned back to Pepper.

Mr. Cubbington-Smith, who had been standing well behind Simon and kind of in the shadows, rushed into the room. In his hands was a long metal bar that looked like a crowbar. Except this bar shone, even in the semi-darkness of the room. It was silver!

For about two seconds my mind clicked on how stupid we had been to go into the tunnels without any silver. We didn't even take garlic. But that's about all the time I had to think about it. Suddenly, a lot of things were happening all at once.

Mr. Cubbington-Smith ran at Lucas with the silver bar raised above his head, poised to come down on the vampire's oversized skull. Lucas let go of Pepper and backed up in a hurry. Then Mr. Cubbington-Smith turned his attention to Annie. She dropped Hal, who thumped noisily to the floor.

The two vampires, who moments before were like a pair of wild animals poised for the kill, were now scrunched down together in the corner. They were actually whimpering.

Suddenly Jaglers laughed. For a second I thought the guy had lost it completely, but there he was laughing like the whole thing was a big joke.

"You fool," he hissed at Mr. Cubbington-Smith. "You think you've won? You've won nothing. Obviously there is no letter, no proof that anyone in my family has ever done wrong."

"That is where you're quite wrong."

I looked over at Simon, but it wasn't him who had spoken. In fact, the voice did not belong to anybody in the room.

Through the doors of the library came Leonard Livermore, moving slowly but with no stoop to his posture. Whatever Jaglers had done to him in the tunnels earlier that night, it hadn't been permanent. Leonard stood erect and smiled at Jaglers as he spoke. "I have the letter. I have had it for over ninety years. I found it in a room in the upper floors of your manor. I decided to hold on to it because I felt that one day it would help me exact my revenge on the Jaglers family. That moment has finally come."

Leonard looked over at where Lucas and Annie were cowering in the corner. "The evil ones knew the story of MacPherson and Lady Pamela. They decided to use the letter to get both Jaglers and Mr. Cubbington-Smith to help them overthrow us."

"A plot that did not work," Simon added. "Earlier this evening, we... eliminated the leader of the renegade group. The revolt is over."

Lucas looked up from where he was crouched in the corner. "You mean . . . Inspector Watts is . . . dead."

Simon did not look at Lucas. He spoke instead to us. "Their leader was a Scotland Yard detective when he was alive. He's been trouble ever since he became vampire." He turned then and looked at Lucas and Annie. "Yes, he is dead."

Leonard crossed the room and handed the letter to me. He couldn't go any closer to Mr. Cubbington-Smith because of the silver bar.

"When this letter is made public," Leonard said, "my revenge will be complete."

Everyone in the room was watching Leonard. Except for one person, that is.

While all of us were distracted, Jaglers lunged at Mr. Cubbington-Smith, knocking him down. The silver bar went clanking harmlessly over the floor and ended up in the opposite corner of the room.

"Get them and get that letter," Jaglers yelled at Lucas and Annie who had recovered enough to scramble back to their feet.

Luckily they weren't the only ones who had returned to normal. Actually, Hal and Pepper didn't seem exactly normal, but they looked a lot better than they had a few minutes before.

"Come on!" I yelled. The silver bar had given me an idea. I ran for the big window at the end of the room. I remembered Hal saying that there was garlic on every window in the manor except our bedrooms. I hoped he was right.

The window was covered by heavy drapes, but if I could get the drapes open fast enough, we'd have a chance. If there was garlic hanging along that window and if we could get under it, it might hold the vampires off for a little while at least.

What happened next wasn't at all what I'd planned. I grabbed the drawstring for the drapes and yanked on it as hard as I could. The drapes snapped open.

As it turned out, it didn't really matter if there was garlic at the window or not. It was daylight outside! Not total, middle-of-the day daylight, but enough light to do some serious damage. When it struck Annie and Lucas, things got completely out of hand.

Both vampires shrieked and seemed to go completely mad in their agony. Their pain must have been unbelievable.

As the day's light burned into their flesh, they screamed again and again—horrible ear-piercing cries unlike anything I'd ever heard. But instead of running away from the light, the pair ran right at it. They must have been driven out of their minds by the pain. That's the only way I can figure it.

The two vampires crashed through the windows and out onto the lawn—into the even brighter light. I wouldn't have wished the results on anyone—not even them. They looked like butter that's been sitting too long in the sun.

They were literally melting right in front of us.

Their faces became unrecognizable mush. Their skin and bones turned from solid to liquid—like a science experiment out of control. As their melted flesh flowed down to the ground like lava, I turned away. I couldn't look any more.

There was still plenty going on in the room. Jaglers and Mr. Cubbington-Smith were in the corner fighting over the silver bar. Both men had their hands on it and each was trying to wrestle it away from the other.

Finally Mr. Cubbington-Smith let go with one hand and drove his fist into Jaglers' face. Jaglers wrenched the bar free and raised it over his head. But before he was able to bring it down, Mr. Cubbington-Smith hit him two more times. Jaglers went crashing back into the fireplace, which unfortunately wasn't lit. It didn't matter though. Jaglers didn't get up. (Or as my brother put it later, he was down for the count. Get it? *Count* Jaglers. Never mind, like I said before, my brother's jokes are mega-stupid.)

When the fight was over, I looked around for Simon or Leonard. There was no sign of either of them. The daylight must have been terrible for them too. We ran into the hall to see where they'd gone. It hadn't been far. Leonard was on his hands and knees near the stairs and Simon was bent over trying to help him up.

Although it was darker in the hall, it was obvious that both of them were suffering horribly. At least their flesh didn't seem to be burning.

We ran to where they were struggling to move. Simon looked at me. His face had none of that annoying superiority that had always bugged me. His eyes were filled with pain and pleading.

"Please," he rasped in a voice I could barely hear. "We must get to somewhere dark—totally dark... or we... will die." He stretched his hand toward me. "Please... help... us."

My mind was racing at something near warp speed. Two vampires—*vampires*—were asking us to save them. But vampires kill people. They kill them in horrible ways. Everyone else must have been having the same thoughts.

"Even if we let them die, it won't mean the end of vampires," Mr. Cubbington-Smith said. "There have been vampires for centuries and they will be around for centuries more."

"They saved our lives," Pepper said.

"Twice," Hal added.

All of them seemed to be saying we should help. One thing was certain—if we didn't do something quickly, Simon and Leonard would die horribly and soon. The house was beginning to fill with light as the sun continued to rise.

"But where... where can we take them? We'll never make it to the tunnels."

"The secret passage!" Hal yelled. "It was pitch black when I was in there."

I took Simon's outstretched hand. "If we help you, will you promise to leave all of us alone—forever?"

"Yes, yes . . . I . . . promise," Simon whispered. "And . . . I'll . . . see to it . . . the others . . . the bad ones . . . leave you alone also. But . . . please, hurry."

"Let's go!" I grabbed Simon by one arm and Pepper grabbed the other. Mr. Cubbington-Smith had to practically carry Leonard. My brother ran up the stairs and into the bedroom Pepper and I shared. When we got there, Hal had already pulled the curtains across the windows. To be honest, I hadn't thought of that.

Hal ran to the fireplace and pushed it open to reveal the secret passage. A little bit of light from the room seeped into the passage. We carried Simon and Leonard inside and laid them gently on the floor.

"Do you want anything?" I asked. "Blankets or anything?"

"No, nothing, thank you," Simon said. "Just go . . . quickly."

I looked at Simon and, for the first time, he tried to smile.

We ran out of the secret passage and closed the door. All four of us stood very still, and no one spoke. We just looked at the fireplace for a long time.

It all seemed too weird. There were two vampires lying in the darkness behind that wall. Yet I wasn't afraid or even nervous. In fact, all I felt was a little sad that we hadn't had time to say goodbye.

21

Party!

We never saw them again. Apparently Simon meant to keep his word. That night after dark, Hal couldn't stand it any more. He pushed open the hidden door to the secret passage. Leonard and Simon were gone. We took a flash-light and looked around the passage to see if there was any trace of them. But there wasn't. At least we didn't see it, at first. Then, just as we were about to leave the passage, Pepper noticed something on the wall.

"Look! Over there."

We focused the flashlight's beam on the spot and, sure enough, Pepper was right. A message had been scrawled on the wall. It was written in something dark, I didn't care to guess what.

"We will never forget your kindness. Thank you and goodbye." The message was signed "We of the After-Dark."

The next day we slept until noon. During lunch with Mr. Cubbington-Smith, we found out that he had decided not to press any charges against Jaglers.

"We'd have to tell the police about the vampires in order to have him charged with anything major," Mr. Cubbington-Smith explained. "And I have a feeling the police might have a little difficulty believing our story. Besides, publication of the letter will be all the satisfaction I require."

"What are you going to do with it?" Pepper asked.

Mr. Cubbington-Smith smiled as he slathered butter on a hot crumpet. "I've already begun. I sent photocopies off to some television news people and a couple of newspapers. A reporter called a little while ago to set up an appointment. She wants to research the whole story of Lady Pamela and MacPherson and the first Jaglers."

"Awright!" Hal yelled. "This calls for a party."

"Quite a good idea, actually," Mr. Cubbington-Smith nodded, "particularly as it's your last night here in London."

I'd completely forgotten that, or maybe in all the excitement I'd just lost track of time. We would be leaving for Stratford-upon-Avon the next day. The party idea did sound like a good one.

"There's one other thing we should think about," Pepper looked at me. "How much of this are we going to tell our parents?"

I shook my head. "I don't know, I really don't."

"I hate to advocate being less than truthful," Mr. Cubbington-Smith said, "but I think in this case the less said, the better."

"Aw, come on," Hal whined, "I say we tell 'em everything. Think of what they're missing."

"Okay," I agreed, "but it would be best if you were the one to tell them. I'm sure you'd tell it best."

"Great!" Hal yelled and charged away from the table. "There's Pepper's mom and dad outside on the lawn. I'll tell them right now."

Mr. Cubbington-Smith looked at me. "Do you think that was wise?"

I grinned at him. "Would you believe Hal if he told you what he's about to tell them?"

"Good point," Mr. Cubbington-Smith smiled and passed the crumpets.

The party idea *would* have been a good one if anyone but Hal had organized it. He decided we should have a vampire party. We all had to wear black capes and these stupid fake fangs he and Mr. Cubbington-Smith found in a convenience store. And we spent the evening drinking strawberry Kool-Aid (blood?) and watching every vampire movie that's ever been made.

And I thought my parents' parties were weird.

Can you believe it?

Don't miss Salt & Pepper's next adventure!

In *Book 2: The Hunk Machine*, Pepper gets bitten by the acting bug! When a Hollywood studio chooses Riverbend as the location for their new western, Pepper decides to try out for a role—and drags Salt along. But it soon becomes clear that this is no normal movie shoot. The producer and his assistant act more like gangsters than moguls. And the stars appear to be hypnotized—like zombies, or robots! Could this have something to do with the weird apparatus Salt spotted at the film headquarters?

When Pepper goes missing, Salt is forced to recruit little brother Hal and his buddies to help. The results are sometimes hilarious, sometimes scary—and always exciting!

Turn the page for a sneak peak at the first chapter of The Salt & Pepper Chronicles, Book 2: The Hunk Machine!

A Creepy House

The house gave me the creeps. It was big and brown and ugly. Some of the upstairs windows were broken and the roof sagged. But the porch was the worst. The paint was faded—where there was paint at all—and the thing looked like it was attached to the rest of the house with a couple of thumbtacks. Oh yeah, and it was scary too. Scary as in it would be the perfect place for an axe murderer to live. As soon as I saw the place, I wanted to get as far away as I could in as short a time as possible. And I would have too, if Pepper hadn't grabbed my arm.

Pepper McKenzie is my best friend . . . well, sometimes. There are two things that aren't so great about having Pepper for a best friend. The first is her nickname, some stupid idea her dad had when she was about three years old. Since we hang around together, guess what a lot of the kids at school call me. Uh-huh...Salt. Get it? Salt and Pepper. People can be so dumb.

But it's the second thing about her that can be *really* irritating. Pepper has a gift for coming up with some pretty crazy ideas and plans. The only thing weirder than some of her ideas is that I usually go along with them. The last time I did that we ended up in London up to our necks in vampires. Yeah, that was fun. This time Pepper said, "We should check out the house where the fire was." Right then and there I should have told her that I had to wash my hair or watch *Oprah* or something. But I didn't.

Which is why we were standing across the street from the creepy house as the sun was going down with Pepper holding onto my arm so I couldn't escape.

"Who...who lives there?" I asked without taking my eyes off the house. I figured she might know since she lives in town. My family and I live in the country a few miles from town, so I don't know everybody who lives in Riverbend.

"New people, I think," she shrugged. "I've never seen 'em."

That *wasn't* what I wanted to hear. "Well, there it is." I tried to sound nonchalant. "You wanted to see it and now you have, so why don't we go to your house and find out if your mom's cinnamon buns are ready."

"My mother isn't making cinnamon buns."

I knew that, but I was willing to try anything. And cinnamon buns are Pepper's favourite.

"Besides," Pepper finally let go of my arm, "I want to get a close-up look."

"But what if . . . ?" I didn't get to finish the sentence. Pepper was already halfway across the street.

"There's probably nobody there right now," I said as I caught up to her on the opposite sidewalk. "I mean with the fire and all."

"Why not?" Pepper argued. "The news said the damage was light. Maybe I'll just go and knock on the door."

It was my turn to grab *her* arm. "I don't think that's such a . . ."

Just then the weirdest thing happened. It was *so* weird that Pepper and I stopped in our tracks and stared at the house. I don't think my mouth was open, but Pepper's was—Grand Canyon open.

I couldn't totally blame her. Four guys had just walked through the front door of the house and onto the porch. And not just any four guys.

These were the four cutest guys I had ever seen. And not one of them looked like an axe murderer.